Rhode Island

Acts Relating to the Public Schools of Rhode Island

Rhode Island

Acts Relating to the Public Schools of Rhode Island

ISBN/EAN: 9783337380557

Printed in Europe, USA, Canada, Australia, Japan

Cover: Foto ©Andreas Hilbeck / pixelio.de

More available books at **www.hansebooks.com**

State of Rhode Island and Providence Plantations.

ACTS

RELATING TO

THE PUBLIC SCHOOLS

OF

RHODE ISLAND,

WITH

REMARKS AND FORMS.

PUBLISHED BY ORDER OF THE GENERAL ASSEMBLY.

PROVIDENCE:
PROVIDENCE PRESS COMPANY, STATE PRINTERS.
1867.

EXTRACTS FROM THE CONSTITUTION OF THE STATE.

ARTICLE I.

DECLARATION OF CERTAIN CONSTITUTIONAL RIGHTS AND PRINCIPLES.

In order effectually to secure the religious and political freedom established by our venerated ancestors, and to preserve the same for our posterity, we do declare that the essential and unquestionable rights and principles hereinafter mentioned, shall be established, maintained and preserved, and shall be of paramount obligation in all legislative, judicial and executive proceedings.

*   *   *   *   *   *   *   *

SECTION 3. Whereas, Almighty God hath created the mind free ; and all attempts to influence it by temporal punishments or burdens, or by civil incapacitations, tend to beget habits of hypocrisy and meanness ; and whereas, a principal object of our venerable ancestors, in their migration to this country and their settlement of this state, was, as they expressed it, to hold forth a lively experiment that a flourishing civil state may stand and be best maintained with full liberty in religious concernments : we, therefore, declare, that no man shall be compelled to frequent or to support any religious worship, place or ministry, whatever, except in fulfilment of his own voluntary contract ; nor enforced, restrained, molested or burdened in his body or goods ; nor disqualified from holding any office ; nor otherwise suffer on account of his religious belief ; and that every man shall be free to worship God according to the dictates of his own conscience, and to profess and by argument to maintain his opinion in matters of religion ; and that the same shall in nowise diminish, enlarge or affect his civil capacity.

ARTICLE XII.

OF EDUCATION.

SECTION 1. The diffusion of knowledge, as well as of virtue among the people, being essential to the preservation of their rights and liberties, it shall be the duty of the general assembly to promote public schools, and to adopt all means which they may deem necessary and proper to secure to the people the advantages and opportunities of education.

Sec. 2.   The money which now is, or which may hereafter be appropriated by law for the establishment of a permanent fund for the support of public schools, shall be securely invested and remain a perpetual fund for that purpose.

Sec. 3.   All donations for the support of public schools or for other purposes of education, which may be received by the general assembly, shall be applied according to the terms prescribed by the donors.

Sec. 4.   The general assembly shall make all necessary provisions by law for carrying this article into effect.   They shall not divert said money or fund from the aforesaid uses, nor borrow, appropriate, or use the same, or any part thereof, for any other purpose, under any pretext whatsoever.

EXTRACTS FROM TITLE THIRD, OF THE REVISED STATUTES.

CHAPTER XIII.

OF THE PERMANENT SCHOOL FUND.

SECTION 1. The general treasurer, with the advice of the governor, shall have full power to regulate the custody and safe-keeping of the fund now constituting the permanent fund for the support of public schools, and to keep the same securely invested in the capital stock of some safe and responsible bank or banks within this state.

SEC. 2. The money that shall be paid into the state treasury by auctioneers for duties accruing to the use of the state, is hereby appropriated, and the same shall annually be added to said school fund for the permanent increase thereof.

SEC. 3. Whenever any money appropriated to any town from the state treasury, for the support of public schools therein, shall have been forfeited by such town, the same shall be added to said school fund, and shall forever remain a part thereof.

SEC. 4. The general treasurer, with the advice of the governor, shall, from time to time, securely invest all sums of money hereby directed to be added to said fund, in the capital stock of some safe and responsible bank or banks within this state.

SEC. 5. The income arising from said fund so invested, shall annually be appropriated for the support of public schools in the several towns.

CHAPTER XIV.

OF THE DEPOSIT FUND.

SECTION 1. The governor, secretary of state and general treasurer are constituted commissioners of the fund received by this state from the United States by virtue of an act of congress, approved June 23, 1836, with full power to regulate the custody and safe-keeping thereof, according to law.

SEC. 2.   The said commissioners may loan, as hereinafter provided, to any town in this state, such portion of said fund as such town would be entitled to receive, according to the ratio of the population of such town under the age of fifteen years, to the whole population of the state, according to the census of the United States next preceding such loan; or they may invest any portion of said fund in the capital stock of some safe and responsible bank or banks within this state.

SEC. 3.   In case the commissioners shall loan any portion of said fund to any town as aforesaid, the treasurer of such town shall give bond to the commissioners, with condition to pay interest on the second Monday in April, on the amount received, at the rate of five per cent. per annum; to pay the whole or such part of the sum loaned as may be required by the commissioners for the purpose of repayment to the United States, when the same shall be demanded; to pay the whole, or such part thereof as shall be required by the general assembly, and when so required; and to apply the money so received for the purpose of education exclusively.

SEC. 4.   The income accruing to the state from said fund shall be set apart, and shall annually be applied to the support of public schools in the several towns.

TITLE XIII.

OF PUBLIC INSTRUCTION.

CHAPTER 58.

OF THE COMMISSIONER OF PUBLIC SCHOOLS.

SECTION
1. Commissioner, how appointed.
2. Duties of the commissioner.
3. To secure uniformity of text-books.

SECTION
4. To prescribe forms for returns.
5. To report to general assembly.

SECTION 1. For the uniform and efficient administration of the provisions of this title, and the supervision and improvement of such schools as may be supported in any manner out of the state treasury, the governor, by and with the advice and consent of the senate, shall annually at the annual general election, appoint a commissioner of public schools, who shall devote his time exclusively to the duties of his office. In case of sickness, temporary absence, or other disability, the governor may appoint a person to act as commissioner during such absence, sickness or disability.

SEC. 2. The commissioner shall visit, annually, every school district in the state, for the purpose of inspecting the schools, and diffusing as widely as possible, by public addresses, and personal communications with school officers, teachers and parents, a knowledge of the defects and desirable improvements in the administration of the system and the government and instruction of the schools; and to defray the travelling expenses of such visits, he shall receive, annually, in addition to his salary, the sum of three hundred dollars.

Sec. 3.   He shall recommend and secure, as far as practicable, a uniformity of text-books in the schools of all the towns; and shall assist in the establishment of, and selection of books for, school libraries.

Sec. 4.   He shall prescribe, from time to time, suitable forms and regulations for carrying the provisions of this title into effect, and for making all reports.

Sec. 5.   He shall, annually, at the adjourned session at Providence, make a report to the general assembly upon the state and condition of the schools and of education, with plans and suggestions for their improvement.

CHAPTER 59.

OF THE APPROPRIATION FOR PUBLIC SCHOOLS.

Section 1.   The sum of fifty thousand dollars shall be annually paid out of the income of the permanent school fund, the deposits fund, and other money in the state treasury for the support of public schools in the several towns, upon the order of the commissioner of public schools.

Sec. 2.   The sum of thirty-five thousand dollars of the amount aforesaid shall be apportioned annually, in May, by the commissioner, among the several towns, in proportion to the number of children therein, under the age of fifteen years, according to the census of the United States then last preceding; and the sum of fifteen thousand dollars shall be apportioned among the several towns in proportion to the number of school districts in each town, corporate or otherwise.

Sec. 3.   The money appropriated from the state shall be denominated " teachers' money," and shall be applied to the wages of teachers, and to no other purpose whatever.

Sec. 4.   No town shall receive any part of the state appropriation, unless it shall raise by tax for the support of public schools, a sum equal to the whole of its proportion of the sum of thirty-five thousand dollars apportioned to such town from the state treasury; and shall appropriate the sum so raised as required by the provisions of this title.

SEC. 5. If any town shall refuse to raise or appropriate the sum required in the section next preceding, on or before the first of July in any year, its proportion of the public money shall be forfeited, and the general treasurer, on being officially informed thereof by the commissioner, shall invest the amount in stocks, to be added to the permanent school fund.

SEC. 6. The commissioner shall draw orders on the general treasurer, in favor of all such towns, for their proportion of the appropriation for public schools, as shall, on or before the first day of July, annually, comply with the conditions of the fourth section of this chapter.

CHAPTER 60.

OF THE POWERS AND DUTIES OF TOWNS, AND OF THE DUTIES OF THE TOWN TREASURER AND TOWN CLERK, RELATING TO PUBLIC SCHOOLS.

SECTION 1. Any town may establish and maintain, without forming districts, a sufficient number of public schools, of different grades, at convenient locations, under the entire management of the school committee.

SEC. 2. Any town may be divided by a vote thereof, into school districts. All existing districts shall continue until legally altered.

SEC. 3. Any town may vote, in a meeting notified for that purpose, to provide school-houses with the necessary fixtures and appendages, in all the districts, if there be districts, at the common expense of the town : *Provided*, that in the latter case, if any district shall provide, at its own expense, a school-house approved by the school committee, such district shall not be liable to be taxed by the town to furnish or repair school-houses for the other districts.

SEC. 5. Each town shall, at its annual town meeting for choice of either state or town officers, choose a school committee, to consist of

2

not less than three residents of said town, and to serve without compensation, unless voted by the town out of the town treasury.

Sec. 5. Any town may appoint or may authorize its school committee to appoint a superintendent of the schools of the town, to perform, under the advice and direction of the committee, such duties and to exercise such powers as the committee may assign to him, and to receive such compensation out of the town treasury as the town may vote.

Sec. 6. The town treasurer shall receive the money due from the state treasury, and shall keep a separate account of all money appropriated by the state or town or otherwise for public schools, and shall pay the same to the order of the school committee.

Sec. 7. The town treasurer shall, within one week after the town meeting at which the committee are elected, submit to them a statement of all moneys in his hands belonging to schools, specifying the sources whence derived, and to what districts, if any, they belong.

Sec. 8. He shall, on or before the first day of July, annually, transmit to the commissioner of public schools a certificate of the amount which the town has voted to raise by tax for the support of public schools for the year; and also a statement of the amount paid out to the order of the school committee, and from what sources it was derived, for the year ending with the thirtieth of April next preceding.

Sec. 9. The town clerk shall record the boundaries of school districts and all alterations thereof, in a book to be kept for that purpose, and shall distribute such school documents and blanks as may be sent to him, to the persons for whom they are intended.

CHAPTER 61.

OF THE POWERS OF SCHOOL DISTRICTS.

SECTION 1. Every school district shall be a body corporate, and shall be known by its number or other suitable or ordinary designation.

Sec. 2. Every school district shall have power to prosecute and defend in all actions, to purchase, receive, hold and convey any real or personal property for school purposes, and to establish and maintain a school library.

Sec. 3.   Every such district may build, purchase, hire and repair school-houses, and supply the same with blackboards, maps, furniture, and other necessary and useful appendages, and may insure the house and appendages against damage by fire : *Provided*, that the erection and repairs of the school-house shall be made according to the plans approved by the school committee or commissioner.

Sec. 4.   Every such district may raise money by tax on the ratable property of the district, to support schools and to carry out the powers given them by any of the provisions of this title : *Provided*, that the amount of the tax shall be approved by the school committee of the town.

Sec. 5.   Every such district shall elect a clerk, either one or three trustees, as they may decide, a treasurer and collector, and may fill vacancies in either of said offices arising from death, declining or refusing to serve, resignation, removal from office, or from the district, or otherwise ; and if an election of any of said officers be not made at the time prescribed for the annual meeting, it may be made at any legally notified meeting afterward.

Sec. 6.   The clerk, collector and treasurer shall have the like power and shall perform like duties as the clerk, collector and treasurer of a town ; but the clerk, collector and treasurer need not give bond unless required by the district.

Sec. 7.   All district taxes shall be collected by the district or town collector, in the same manner as town taxes are collected.

Sec. 8.   Any district may vote to place the collection of any district tax or rate bill in the hands of the collector of town taxes, who shall thereupon, without any new bond or engagement, be fully authorized to proceed and collect the same.

Sec. 9.   If any school district shall neglect to organize, or if organized, shall, for any space of six months, neglect to establish a school and employ a teacher, the school committee of the town may themselves, or by an agent, establish a school in the district school-house, or elsewhere, in their discretion, and employ a teacher.

Sec. 10.   Any district may, with the consent of the committee, devolve all the powers and duties relating to public schools in the district on the committee.

CHAPTER 62.

OF DISTRICT MEETINGS.

SECTION 1. Notice of the time, place and object of holding the first meeting of a district for organization, or for a meeting to choose officers or transact other business, in case there be no trustees authorized to call a meeting, shall be given by the school committee of the town, at such time, and in such manner as they may deem proper.

SEC. 2. Every school district, when organized, shall hold an annual meeting in the month of March, April or May of each year, for choice of officers and transaction of any other business relating to schools.

SEC. 3. The trustees may call a special meeting for election, or other business at any time, and shall call one to be held within seven days, on the written request of any five qualified voters, stating the object for which they wish it called; and if the trustees neglect or refuse to call a special meeting when requested, the school committee may call it, and fix the time therefor.

SEC. 4. District meetings shall be held at the school-house unless otherwise ordered by the district. If there be no school-house, or place appointed by the district, the trustees, or if there be no trustees, the school committee shall determine the place, which shall always be within the district.

SEC. 5. Notice of the time and place of every annual meeting, and of the time, place and object of every special meeting, shall be given for five days inclusive, before holding the same.

SEC. 6. The trustees shall give notice of a district meeting, either by publishing the same in a newspaper published in the district, or by putting the notice on the district school-house, or on a sign-post within the district; or if there be no newspaper, school-house or sign-post, then in such manner as the school committee may direct: *Provided*, that the district may, from time to time, prescribe the mode of notifying meetings, and the trustees shall conform thereto.

SEC. 7. Every district meeting may appoint a moderator, and adjourn from time to time.

SEC. 8. Every person residing in the district may vote in district meetings, to the same extent and with the same restrictions as he would at the time be qualified to vote in town meeting, but no person shall vote upon any question of taxation of property, or expending money raised thereby, unless he shall have paid, or be liable to pay, a portion of the tax.

SEC. 9.   The clerk of the district shall record the number and names of the persons voting, and on which side of the question, at the request of any qualified voter.

CHAPTER 63.

OF JOINT SCHOOL DISTRICTS.

SECTION 1.   Any two or more adjoining primary school districts in the same or adjoining towns, may, by a concurrent vote, agree to establish a secondary or grammar-school, for the older and more advanced children of such districts.

SEC. 2.   Such associating districts shall constitute a school district for all the purposes of providing a school-house, fuel, furniture and apparatus, and for the election of a board of trustees, to consist of one member from each associating district, and for the laying of a tax for school purposes, and fixing rates of tuition, with all the rights and privileges of a school district so far as the secondary school is concerned.

SEC. 3.   The time and place for the meeting for organization of such associating districts may be fixed by the school committees, and any one or more of the associating districts may delegate to the trustees of the secondary school, the care and management of its primary school.

SEC. 4.   The school committee of the town or towns in which such secondary school shall be established, shall draw an order in favor of the trustees of said school, to be paid out of the public money appropriated to each district interested in the secondary school, in proportion to the number of scholars from each.

SEC. 5.   Any two or more adjoining school districts in the same town may, by concurrent vote, with the approbation of the school committee, unite together and be consolidated into one district, for the purpose of supporting public schools; and such consolidated district shall have all the powers of a single district.

SEC. 6.   Such consolidated district shall be entitled to receive the same proportion of public money the districts would receive if not united.

SEC. 7.   The mode of organizing such consolidated district and calling the first meeting thereof, shall be regulated or prescribed by the school committee.

SEC. 8.   Two or more contiguous districts, or parts of districts in adjoining towns, may be formed into a joint school district by the school committees of such towns concurring therein; and all joint districts which have been or shall be formed, may by them be altered or discontinued.

SEC. 9.   The meeting for organization of such joint district shall be called by notice signed by the school committees of such towns, and set up in one or more places in each district, or part of a district.

SEC. 10.   Such joint district shall have all the powers of a single school district, and shall be regulated in the same manner, and shall be subject to the supervision and management of the school committee of the town in which the school is located.

SEC. 11.   A whole district making a portion of such joint district, shall be entitled to its portion of public money, in the same manner as if it remained a single district; and when part of a district is taken to form a portion of such joint district, the school committee shall assign to it its reasonable proportion.

SEC. 12.   When any two or more districts shall be consolidated into one, the new district shall own all the corporate property of the several districts.

SEC. 13.   When a district is divided, and a portion taken from it, the funds and property, or the income and proceeds thereof, shall be divided among the several parts, in such manner as the school committee of the town or towns to which the districts belong, may determine.

SEC. 14.   When a part of one district is added to another district or part of a district owning a school-house or other property, such part shall pay to the district or part of a district to which it is added, if demanded, such sum as the school committee may determine.

CHAPTER 64.

OF THE LEVY OF DISTRICT TAXES, AND OF RATE BILLS FOR TUITION.

SECTION 1.   District taxes shall be levied on the ratable property of the district, according to its value in the town assessment then last made, unless the district shall direct taxes to be levied upon the next town assessment; and no notice thereof shall be required to be given by the trustees.

SEC. 2.   The trustees of any school district, if unable to agree with the parties interested, with regard to the valuation of any property in such district, shall call upon one or more of the town assessors not interested, and not residing in the district, to assess the value of such property so situated, in the following cases, namely: When any real estate in the district is assessed in the town tax bill with real estate out of the district, so that there is no distinct or separate value upon it; when any person possessing personal property shall remove into the district after the last town assessment; when a division and apportionment of a tax shall become necessary by reason of the death of any person, or the sale of such property; when a person has invested personal property in real estate, and shall call upon the trustees to place a value thereon; and when property shall have been omitted in the town valuation.

SEC. 3.   The assessors shall give notice of such assessment, by putting up notices for ten days in three of the most public places in or near the district; and after notice is given as aforesaid, no person neglecting to appear before the assessors shall have any remedy for being over-taxed.

SEC. 4.   If a district tax shall be voted, assessed and approved of, and a contract legally entered into under it, or such contract be legally entered into without such vote, assessment or approval, and said district shall thereafter neglect or refuse to proceed and collect a tax, the commissioner, after notice to and hearing of the parties, may approin assessors to assess a tax, and may issue a warrant to the collector of the district, or to a collector by him appointed, authorizing and requiring him to proceed and collect said tax.

SEC. 5. Errors in assessing a tax may be corrected, or the tax reässessed in such manner as may be directed or approved by the commissioner.

SEC. 6. When any person who has paid a tax for building or repairing a school-house in one district, shall, by alteration of the boundaries thereof, become liable to pay a tax in any other district, if such person cannot agree with the district, such abatement of the tax may be made as the school committee, or in case of a district composed from different towns, as the commissioner may deem just and proper.

SEC. 7. When a joint district shall vote to build or repair a school-house by tax, the amount of the tax and the plan and specifications of the building and repairs shall be approved by the school committees of the several towns, or by the commissioner.

SEC. 8. In case of assessing a tax by a joint or secondary district, if the town assessments be made upon different principles, or the relative value be not the same, the relative value and proportion shall be ascertained by one or more persons, to be appointed by the commissioner, and the assessment shall be made accordingly.

SEC. 9. Any school district, in addition to the money received from the state and town appropriations, may fix, or authorize its trustees to fix, subject to the approval of the school committee of the town, a rate of tuition, to be paid by the persons attending school, or by their parents, employers or guardians, towards the expense of fuel, books and other expenses, including estimated deficiencies of payments.

SEC. 10. The rate of tuition so fixed, shall not exceed one dollar for each scholar for any term of eleven weeks, except in towns or districts where different grades of schools are established; and in such towns or districts the rate for higher grades shall not exceed two dollars for each scholar, for the same time.

SEC. 11. In all cases in which there is no district organization, the school committee may fix the rate of tuition.

SEC. 12. The district, the trustees, or committee, shall exempt from the payment of any such rate bill any person whom they shall consider unable to pay the same.

SEC. 13. All such rate bills may be required to be paid in advance, or may be delivered to the town or district collector, and may be by them collected in the same manner as town taxes are collected.

SEC. 14. The trustees may prescribe and collect a rate, in their discretion, sufficient to keep the school for the four months required by law, without any vote of the district.

CHAPTER 65.

OF THE TRUSTEES OF SCHOOL DISTRICTS.

SEC. 1.   The trustees of the school districts shall have the custody of the scool-house and other district property, and shall employ one or more qualified teachers for every fifty scholars in average daily attendance.

SEC. 2.   They shall provide school-rooms and fuel, and shall visit the schools twice at least during each term, and notify the committee or superintendent of the time of opening and closing the school.

SEC. 3.   They shall see that the scholars are properly supplied with books, and in case they are not, and the parents, guardians or masters have been notified thereof by the teacher, shall provide the same at the expense of the district, and add the same to the next rate bill of such person.

SEC. 4.   They shall make out the tax bill and rate bills for tuition against the person liable to pay the same, and deliver the same to the collector with a warrant by them signed annexed thereto, requiring him to collect and pay over the same to the treasurer of the district.

SEC. 5.   They shall make returns to the school committee in manner and form prescribed by them or by the commissioner, or as may be required by law, and perform all other lawful acts required of them by the district, or necessary to carry into full effect the powers and duties of districts.

SEC. 6.   Trustees shall receive no compensation for services out of the money received from either the state or town appropriations, nor in any way unless raised by tax by the district.

CHAPTER 66.

OF THE POWERS AND DUTIES OF SCHOOL COMMITTEES.

3

SECTION 1. The school committee of each town shall choose a chairman and clerk, either of whom may sign any orders or official papers, and may be removed at the pleasure of said committee.

SEC. 2. They shall hold at least four stated meetings, viz.: on the second Mondays of January, April, July and October, in every year, and as much oftener as the state of the schools shall require. A majority of the number elected shall constitute a quorum unless the committee consist of more than six, when four shall be a quorum, but any number may adjourn.

SEC. 3. They may alter and discontinue school districts, and shall settle their boundaries when undefined or disputed; but no new district shall be formed with less than forty children, between the ages of four and sixteen, unless with the approbation of the commissioner.

SEC. 4. They shall locate all school-houses, and shall not abandon or change the site of any without good cause.

SEC. 5. In case the school committee shall fix upon a location for a school-house in any district, and the district shall have passed a vote to erect a school-house, or where there is no district organization and the committee shall fix upon a location for a school-house, and the proprietor of the land shall refuse to convey the same, or cannot agree with the district for the price thereof, the school committee of their own motion, or upon application of the district, shall be authorized to appoint three disinterested persons, who shall notify the parties and decide upon the valuation of the land; and upon the tender, or payment of the sum so fixed upon to the proprietor, the title to the land so fixed upon by the school committee, not exceeding one half of an acre, shall vest in the district for the purpose of maintaining a school-house and the necessary appendages thereof.

SEC. 6. An appeal in such cases shall be allowed to the court of common pleas in the same manner and with the same effect, as is provided by law, in cases of laying out highways.

SEC. 7. The committee shall examine by themselves or by some one or more persons by them appointed, all applicants for the situation of teachers in the public schools of the town, and shall after five days notice in writing annul the certificates of such as prove unqualified or will not conform to the regulations of the committee, and in such case shall give immediate notice thereof to the trustee of the district in which such teacher is employed.

SEC. 8. They shall visit by one or more of their number every public school in the town, at least twice during each term, once within two weeks of its opening, and once within two weeks of its close, at which visits they shall examine the register and other matters touching the school-house, library, studies, books, discipline, modes of teaching and improvement of the schools.

SEC. 9. The committee may employ some person, of or not of their number, to perform the duty required of them by the next preceding section, and such person shall receive such compensation as the committee may allow, out of the money raised by the town, or as the town may allow.

SEC. 10. They shall make and cause to be put up in each school-house rules and regulations for the attendance and classification of the pupils, for the introduction and use of text-books, and works of reference, and for the instruction, government and discipline of the public schools, and shall prescribe the studies to be pursued therein.

SEC. 11. They shall suspend during pleasure, or expel during the school term, all pupils found guilty of incorrigibly bad conduct, or violation of the school regulations, and shall readmit them on satisfactory evidence of amendment.

SEC. 12. They shall fill any vacancy in the committee occasioned by the death, declining or refusing to serve, resignation, removal from office or from the town, or otherwise.

SEC. 13. Where a town is not divided into districts, or shall vote in a meeting duly notified for that purpose, to provide schools, without reference to such division, the committee shall manage and regulate said schools, and draw all orders for the payment of their expenses.

SEC. 14. When the public schools are maintained by district organization, the committee shall apportion, as early as practicable in each year, among the districts, the town's proportion of the sum of thirty-five thousand dollars received from the state, one half equally, and the other half according to the average daily attendance of the schools of the preceding year.

SEC. 15. When the town is divided into school districts having the management of their own concerns, the committee shall apportion equally among all the districts of the town, the town's proportion of the sum of fifteen thousand dollars received from the state.

SEC. 16. They shall apportion the money received from the town, from the registry tax, from funds or other grants, either equally or in such proportion as the town may direct, and for want of such direction, then in such manner as they deem best.

SEC. 17. They shall, immediately after making the apportionment among the several districts as provided in the three sections next preceding, give notice to the trustees of the amounts so apportioned to each district.

SEC. 18. They shall draw an order on the town treasurer in favor of such districts only, as shall have made a return to them in manner and form prescribed by them or by the commissioner, or as may be required by law, from which it shall appear that for the year ending on the first of May previous, one or more public schools have been kept for at least four months by a qualified teacher in a school-house approved by the committee or commissioner, and that the money designated "teachers' money," received the year previous, has been applied to the wages of teachers and to no other purpose.

SEC. 19. Such orders may be made payable to the trustees or their order, or to the district treasurer, or teacher; and if the treasurer receive the money, he shall pay it out to the order of the trustees.

SEC. 20. The committee shall not give any such order until they are satisfied the services have actually been performed for which the money is to be paid; and the register, properly kept, has been deposited with the committee, or with some person by them appointed to receive the same.

SEC. 21. At the end of the school year, any money appropriated to any district which shall be forfeited, and the forfeiture not remitted, or which shall remain unexpended, may be divided by the committee among the districts the following year.

SEC. 22. The committee shall prepare, and submit annually, a report to the commissioner, on or before the first day of July, in manner and form by him prescribed; also a written or printed report to the town at the annual town meeting, when the school committee is chosen, setting forth their doings, the state and condition of the schools, and plans for their improvement, which report, unless printed, shall be read in open town meeting, and they shall transmit a copy thereof to the commissioner, on or before the first day of July in each year.

SEC. 23. The committee may reserve annually out of the public appropriation, a sum not exceeding twenty dollars, to defray the expense of printing their report.

SEC. 24. The school committee of any town, or trustees of any school dirstrict, may make arrangements with the school committee of any adjacent town, or trustees of any adjacent district, for the attendance of such children as will be better accommodated in the public schools of such adjacent town or district, and may pay such portion of the expense as may be just and proper.

When, however, children attend in the public schools of such adjacent town or district without such arrangements with the school committee or the trustees, it shall be the duty of the trustees where they so attend, to render at the end of each and every school term to the trustees of the district where such children belong, an accurate account of such attendance; and in estimating the "average daily attendance" such attendance shall only be reckoned for the district where such children belong.

CHAPTER 67.

OF TEACHERS.

SECTION 1. No person shall be employed in any town to teach as principal or assistant in any school, supported entirely or in part by the public money, unless he has a certificate of qualification, signed either by the school committee of the town, or by some person or persons appointed by said committee.

SEC. 2. Such certificate, unless annulled, if signed by the school committee, shall be valid within the town for one year.

SEC. 3. The school committee shall not sign any certificate of qualification unless the person named in the same shall produce evidence of good moral character, and be found on examination qualified to teach the English language, arithmetic, penmanship, and the rudiments of geography and history, and to govern a school.

SEC. 4. The school committee of any town may dismiss any teacher who shall refuse to conform to the regulations by them made, or for other just cause, and in such case shall give immediate notice to the trustees of the district.

SEC. 5. Every teacher in any public school shall keep a register of all the scholars attending said school, their sex, ages, names of parents or guardians, the time when each enters and leaves the school, the daily attendance; together with the days of the month on which the school is visited by any officer connected with public schools, and shall prepare the district's return to the school committee of the town, if requested to do so by the trustees.

SEC. 6. Every teacher shall aim to implant and cultivate in the minds of all children committed to his care, the principles of morality and virtue.

CHAPTER 68.

OF LEGAL PROCEEDINGS RELATING TO PUBLIC SCHOOLS.

SECTION 1.   Any person may appeal from the decision or doings of any school committee, district meeting, trustees, or in any other matter arising under this title, to the commissioner of public schools, who is hereby authorized and required to examine and decide the same without cost to the parties.

SEC. 2.   The commissioner may, and if requested, on hearing of such appeal, by either party, shall, lay a statement of the facts of the case before some one of the justices of the supreme court, whose decision shall be final.

SEC. 3.   The commissioner may prescribe from time to time rules regulating the time and manner of making such appeals, and to prevent their being made for trifling and frivolous pretences.

SEC. 4.   Any persons having any matter of dispute between them arising under this title, may agree in writing to submit the same to the adjudication of said commissioner, and his decision therein shall be final.

SEC. 5.   If no appeal be taken from a vote of a district relating to the ordering of a tax or rate bill, or from the proceedings of the officers of the district in assessing the same, or if on appeal, such proceedings are confirmed, the same shall not again be questioned before any court of law or magistrate whatever: *Provided*, that this section shall not be construed to dispense with legal notice of the meeting, or with the votes or proceedings being approved by the school committee or commissioner, whenever the same is required by law.

SEC. 6.   In any civil suit before any court, against any school officer, for any matter which might by this chapter have been heard and decided by the commissioner, no cost shall be taxed for the plaintiff, if the court are of opinion that such officer acted in good faith.

SEC. 7.   Any inhabitant of a district, or person liable to pay taxes therein, may be allowed by any court to answer a suit brought against the district, on giving security for costs, in such manner as the court may direct.

SEC. 8.   The school-house lot, with the school-house and appendages, shall be exempt from attachment, or sale on execution in any suit against the district.

SEC. 9. When judgment shall be recovered in any court of record against any school district, the court rendering judgment shall order a warrant to be issued, if no appeal be taken, to the assessors of taxes of the town in which such district is situated, or in case a joint district, composed of parts of towns, then to one or more of the assessors of each town, with or without designating them, requiring them to assess upon the ratable property in said district, a tax sufficient to pay the debts or damages, costs, interest, and a sum in the discretion of the court sufficient to defray the expenses of assessment and collection. Said assessors shall, without a new engagement, proceed to assess the same, giving notice as in case of other district taxes.

SEC. 10. Said warrant shall also contain a direction to the collector of the town, or in case of a joint district, then to the collector of either town the court may direct, requiring him to collect said tax; and said warrant, with the assessment annexed thereto, shall be a sufficient authority for the collector, without a special engagement, to proceed and collect the same with the same power as in case of a town tax; and when collected, he shall pay over the same to the parties to whom it may belong, and the surplus, if any, to the district. And the court may require a bond of the collector at their discretion.

SEC. 11. When any writ, summons, or other process shall issue against any school district in any civil suit, the same may be served on the treasurer or clerk, and if there are no such officers to be found, the officer charged with the same may post up a certified copy thereof on the door of the school-house, and if there is no school-house, then in some most public place in the district, and the same when proved to the satisfaction of the court, shall constitute a sufficient service thereof.

SEC. 12. Inhabitants of school districts, or persons paying taxes therein, shall be competent witnesses in all civil and criminal cases, notwithstanding such interest, if not otherwise disqualified.

SEC. 13. The record of a clerk of a district, that a meeting has been duly or legally notified, shall be *prima facie* evidence that it has been notified as the law requires. The clerk shall procure, at the expense of the district, a suitable bound book for keeping the records therein.

SEC. 14. The commissioner shall hear and decide all appeals, and may remit all fines, penalties and forfeitures incurred by any town, district or person under any of the provisions of this title, except the forfeiture incurred by any town for not raising its proportion of money as specified in section four, of chapter fifty-nine of this title.

CHAPTER 69.

NORMAL SCHOOL AND SCHOOL JOURNAL.

SECTION 1. There shall be established, as hereinafter provided, one normal school, to be called the State Normal School, for the training of teachers in the art of governing and instructing the common schools of the state.

SEC. 2. Said school shall be under the supervision of a board of trustees, to be called the trustees of the normal school. This board shall consist of the governor (*ex officio*) president, the commissioner of the public schools (*ex officio*) secretary, and five other members, one from each county in the state; who shall, from and after their first appointment by the general assembly, in grand committee, be annually appointed by the general assembly, in grand committee, at its May session, in the order hereinafter provided. Of these five, two shall hold their office for three years, two for two years, and one for one year; the term of office of each to be determined by lot or otherwise; the vacancies to be filled by appointment by the general assembly, in grand committee, for the residue of the term which shall so become vacant.

SEC. 3. It shall be the duty of said board to meet quarterly, at such time and place as they may determine; to keep a record of their proceedings, and to report the same annually, in connection with the report of the commissioner of public schools, to the general assembly, at its January session. It shall also be the duty of said board to visit, by one or more of their number, said school, at least once during each term, and to report its condition to the full board, at its next succeeding quarterly session. The expenses necessarily incurred by said board of trustees, or any one of their number, in the discharge of official duties, shall be defrayed out of the fund hereby appropriated for the support of said school; but they shall receive no compensation for their services. A majority of said board shall constitute a quorum for the transaction of business; but any number may adjourn.

SEC. 4. To said board of trustees shall be committed the location of said school, the application of the funds for the support thereof, the appointment of the principal and teachers, and the power of removing the same for proper cause; the power to prescribe rules for its management, and to grant diplomas. Said trustees are hereby authorized, from and after the summer term of the year one thousand eight hundred and sixty-one, (1861,) to change the location of said normal school, from time to time, as they may deem best for the interest of said school, and for the accommodation of the pupils in the different parts of the state; provided, suitable buildings and fixtures are furnished without expense to the state.

SEC. 5. The number of pupils shall not at any time exceed one hundred and twenty-five. All applicants must declare, in writing, their intention to qualify themselves for teachers in the state; they must present to the principal a certificate of good moral character, and of such other personal qualifications as ought to be found in every instructor of the young. They must be, if males, at least sixteen; and, if females, at least fifteen years of age. They must pass a satisfactory written and oral examination, by the principal, in reading, writing, spelling, arithmetic, geography and grammar, and must remain in the school at least one full term.

SEC. 6. The trustees shall apportion for each county, from the whole number of applicants who are qualified, in accordance with the requirements of the next preceding section, a number of pupils proportionate to the population of each county. If there shall not be a sufficient number of applicants from any county to fill the number of appointments, allowed to each county, the trustees shall fill the vacancy from among the whole number of remaining applicants. To all pupils so admitted to the school, the tuition and all the privileges of the school shall be gratuitous.

SEC. 7. A sum not exceeding two thousand five hundred dollars, is hereby annually appropriated for the establishment and support of said school.

SEC. 8. A sum, not exceeding three hundred dollars, is hereby annually appropriated for the purpose of distributing in the several school districts, under the direction of the commissioner of public schools, some educational journal, published in this state.

SEC. 9. All other acts in relation to the normal school, teachers' institute, and addresses, in the several school districts, are hereby repealed.

SEC. 10. This act shall take effect immediately after its passage.

CHAPTER 70.

OF TRUANT CHILDREN AND ABSENTEES FROM SCHOOL.

SECTION 1. Each of the several towns of this state is authorized and empowered to make all needful provisions and arrangements concerning habitual truants, and children between the ages of six and sixteen years not attending school, without any regular and lawful employment, and growing up in ignorance, and, also, such ordinances and by-laws respecting such children as shall be deemed most conducive to their welfare, and the good order of such town.

SEC. 2. There shall be annexed to such ordinances suitable penalties not exceeding, for any one breach thereof, a fine of ten dollars, or, instead of such fine, the offender may be committed for a period not exceeding one year to any such institution of instruction, or suitable situation, as may be provided for that purpose under the authority given in the section next preceding: *Provided*, that no child shall be sent to any place used for the reception of criminals, or to any reform school.

SEC. 3. Such ordinances and by-laws shall not take effect until approved by the commissioner of public schools.

SEC. 4. The several towns, availing themselves of the provisions of this chapter shall appoint, at their annual town meetings, or annually by their town councils, three or more persons, who alone shall be authorized to make the complaints, in case of violation of said ordinances or by-laws, to the justice of the peace, or court which, by said ordinances shall have jurisdiction in the matter; and said persons thus appointed shall alone have authority to carry into execution the judgment of said justice or court.

CHAPTER 71.

GENERAL PROVISIONS RELATING TO PUBLIC SCHOOLS.

SECTION 1. No person shall be excluded from any public school in the district to which such person belongs, if the town is divided into districts, or, if not so divided, from the nearest public school on account of being over fifteen years of age, nor except by force of some general regulation applicable to all persons under the same circumstances, and in no sase on account of the inability of himself, his parents, guardian or employer, to pay any rate bill, tax or assessment whatever.

SEC. 2.   All school officers appointed under the provisions of this title, except the moderator of a district meeting, shall take an engagement before some judge, senator, justice or warden, notary, town clerk, member of the town council, or chairman or clerk of the school committee, to support the constitution of the United States, the constitution and laws of this state, and faithfully to discharge the duties of their several offices, so long as they continue therein.

SEC. 3.   The clerk of the district may take the engagement in open district meeting, before the moderator, or any magistrate present, and the clerk's record that any district officer has been duly engaged, shall be *prima facie* evidence thereof; and all district school officers may be engaged by the clerk of the district.

SEC. 4.   If any school officer shall not take such engagement within a reasonable time, he shall be fined one dollar, but all acts of such officers otherwise lawful, shall be valid from the time of their election or appointment.

SEC. 5.   All officers under the provisions of this title shall, without a new engagement, hold their offices until the time of the next annual election or appointment for such office, and until other persons are appointed in their places.

SEC. 6.   Any officer who shall make any false certificate, or appropriate any public school money to any purpose not authorized by law, or who shall refuse for a reasonable charge to give certified copies of any official paper, or to account or deliver to his successor, any accounts, papers or money in his hands, or shall wilfully or knowingly refuse to perform any duty of his office, or violate any provisions of any law regulating public schools, except where a particular penalty may be prescribed, shall be fined not exceeding five hundred dollars, or imprisoned not exceeding six months, and shall besides be liable to suit for damages by any person injured thereby.

SEC. 7.   Any such officer refusing to account or to deliver over any accounts, papers or moneys to his successor in office, shall, in addition to the foregoing penalty, be liable to a suit therefor, to be brought by such successor.

SEC. 8.   Any school or asylum incorporated by or receiving aid from the state, either by direct grant or by exemption from taxation, shall be liable to be examined or visited by the school committee of the town or city in which such institution is situated, whenever the committee shall see fit.

SEC. 9.   Any such institution refusing to admit such committee, when requested, shall be fined one hundred dollars; and their exemption from taxation shall thereafter cease and be determined.

SEC. 10.   If any person shall keep any swine, of any description, in any pen or other inclosure, or who shall keep or suffer to be kept any other nuisance within one hundred feet of any district schoolhouse, or within one hundred feet of any fence inclosing the yard of any such school-house, he shall be fined twenty dollars, one half thereof to and for the use of the school district in which said offence is committed, and the other half thereof to and for the use of the state.

SEC. 11.   In the construction of this title, except in the construction of the seventieth chapter thereof, and the eighth and ninth sections of this chapter, the word town shall include the city of Providence only so far as to entitle said city to a distributive share of the public money, upon making a report to the commissioner in the same manner as the school committees of other towns are required to do.

SEC. 12.   The public schools in said city shall continue as heretofore to be governed according to such ordinances and regulations as the proper city authorities may from time to time adopt.

CHAPTER 616.

AN ACT TO PROVIDE COMMON SCHOOLS TEACHERS WITH ADDITIONAL NORMAL INSTRUCTION.

It is enacted by the General Assembly as follows :

SECTION 1. The General Treasurer shall pay yearly on receiving an order to that effect from the Commissioner of Public Schools, to the Trustees of the Academy at East Greenwich, and to any other Academies or High Schools, possessing, in the opinion of the Commissioner, suitable appliances for furnishing " Normal instruction," the sum of fifteen dollars, ($15,) for each scholar who shall have been in said Academy or Academies and High Schools, instructed for not less than one term, in accordance with the requirements of this act, in the studies taught in the common schools of this State and in the science of common school teaching, provided the whole amount thus appropriated shall not exceed fifteen hundred dollars ($1500) per year.

SEC. 2. The Commissioner shall not give his order for any amount, as above provided, until the Trustees of said Academy or Academies and High Schools shall have furnished him satisfactory evidence that a class, not to exceed forty in number in any Academy or High Schools, have been instructed with special reference to teaching in the common schools, and said trustees shall obtain from each person thus taught, a certificate, stating his or her intention to become a teacher, and shall furnish the same to the Commissioner of Public Schools, and they shall also furnish him a certificate stating such persons' qualifications for teaching, to the satisfaction of said School Commissioner ; provided, that in case the number so instructed shall exceed one hundred persons, the aforesaid sum of $1500 shall be divided pro rata among the whole number thus taught.

REMARKS.

REMARKS

ON SOME OF THE PROVISIONS OF THE SCHOOL LAW, AND ON THE DUTIES OF DIFFERENT OFFICERS AND BODIES CORPORATE UNDER THEM.

TOWNS.

In order to receive its allowance from the State treasury, a town must first vote to raise the amount the law requires; and if voted annually, the vote must be passed on or before July 1st, in every year. But an appropriation may be made by a standing by-law, under which the town treasury may every year make the necessary appropriation.

The revised statutes require each town to raise one-half of the amount it receives from the division of the thirty-five thousand dollars. This will add to the tax of only about five towns in the State, and but a very small sum annually to each of their tax bills. This change in the law should be especially noted, or some of these towns may, by neglect, forfeit the whole money they now receive from the State. Let them and all the towns remember that they can hardly expend too much money on their schools, if they expend it under the most rigid system of supervision; and when such intelligent control and visitation are not demanded, almost the whole of any small amount of money raised for schools will be comparatively a waste.

It is believed that where a town is divided into districts, and each district has trustees to manage its own local affairs, it will be better to have the town's committee a small one, provided competent persons can be obtained to undertake it. Their duties are to examine teachers, visit, and have a supervision of the schools. There is danger that a large committee will not meet often, and that they will attempt to perform too many of their duties by small sub-committees of one or more. The delegation by the whole committee, to each member, of the power to manage some particular district, was one great cause of the inefficiency of the former system. The examination of teachers should, in all cases where it is possible, be done by the whole committee; and incompetent persons will be less likely to apply to the whole committee, than to a single member, to be examined, and the persons appointed to visit particular schools, should always make specific reports to the whole board at their monthly or quarterly sessions. In this way alone can the annual report of the school committee be made up properly and as fully as is necessary. Special attention to the duties of examination of schools alone can fit the committee to make such annual communication to the people of the town on the subject of their schools, as shall be of greatest service to them. This annual report should by all means be printed and circulated among all the citizens of the town. The mothers and the sisters of the scholars should see it as well as the fathers and voters, and the only way in which they can all enjoy this privilege is to have it printed and at least one copy furnished to each family in the town. It is then easy to make all citizens acquainted with the workings of our school system, and to induce them carefully to guard the expenditures made for the common benefit.

By the new act, a town may appoint or authorize its committee to appoint a superintendent of schools. In such case the superintendent will perform the duties of examining teachers, visiting schools, and such other duties as the committee may assign him. This will relieve the committee of a very laborious portion of their duties, and at the same time secure a far more accurate and careful comparison of one school with all the others in the town. It will also give far more regularity and systematic teaching in all the schools, and will aid the teachers in many cases of government and discipline where they greatly need the benefit not only of greater authority, but a wiser and more experienced judgment.

Several towns have already adopted this mode of conducting their schools, and not one is known to have regretted the progressive step. A good way might be for two or three towns to unite and employ a man who should devote his whole time to their schools, paying him in proportion to the time actually spent in the schools of each town. The only objection that could be made to such an arrangement would probably be the mutual jealousies of towns. But it is to be hoped that these will not stand in the way of some method of bringing about the appointment of superintendents of schools in every town in the State.

The town treasurer should, as soon as the State money is apportioned, which is to be done in May, and as soon as the school committee have made their report and the town has voted to raise what the law

TOWN TREASURER.

requires, apply to the commissioner for an order for his town's portion. If the town appropriation be made by standing by-law instead of an annual vote, he may apply immediately, provided the school committee have made the report the law requires. Some towns make a practice of depositing their school money in some bank, which will pay them a low rate of interest. But it should be always subject to order.

If the treasurer is newly elected, or his election not generally known, it may be well for him to procure from the town clerk a certificate to the fact of his being town treasurer.

He is to keep a separate account of all school moneys, and is, within one week after the annual town meeting, to furnish the school committee with a particular account of all school moneys in his hands, the sources from which derived, &c. He can only pay out the school money, (whether derived from the State, town, or registry tax,) to orders signed by the chairman or clerk of the school committee, and if he pays it out or appropriates it otherwise, he would be liable to the penalty of the law.

The town treasurer, to obtain the State appropriation, should furnish to the commissioner a certificate substantially in the following form, signed by himself, or the town clerk :—

Town of   A. D. 18   .

I certify, that, in addition to the funds received from the State, and to the unexpended school moneys of last year, received from all sources, this town has, by vote passed in legal town meeting, appropriated the sum of   dollars, to be paid out of the town treasury, for the support of public schools in this town for the present year according to law.

A. B.,
                Town Treasurer or Town Clerk.

To C. D., Commissioner of Public Schools.

It will be seen that, by the revised statutes, the town treasurer is obliged to make a statement to the several school districts of the town, of the amount of money apportioned by the school committee of the town to such districts; and he is also to submit to the commissioner of public schools a statement of all money expended for the public schools of the town, and the sources whence it is derived. The object of these provisions plainly is to enable each of the separate and independent officers of the public school system to understand how much money every district is by law entitled to, and to be able to lay before the people at proper times a full and accurate account of the mode of its expenditure. Provisions so salutary and reasonable ought not to be neglected; and if they are neglected, it is not certain but that the town would be deprived of its part of the public money, or at least delayed or put to expense to obtain it.

SCHOOL COMMITTEES.

The school committee should first be engaged, and then elect their chairman and clerk; and these officers are liable to be removed at the pleasure of the committee. It would be well to have the certificate of their own election and engagement made upon the record book itself, as loose papers are more liable to be lost. [See form.]

The number of the school committee, three or more, may be fixed at each annual town election. If the town fails to elect at the annual town meeting, the town council must elect them at its *next* meeting. Otherwise the old committee will hold over. But any town may vote to delegate to the council the power of appointing the committee.

Vacancies.—If any member of the committee resigns, the rest (if there be a quorum) may supply the vacancy. If so many resign or refuse to serve as not to leave a quorum, the vacancy must, as in case of other town officers, be supplied by the town council, until the next town meeting.

Meetings.—They should hold meetings at least quarterly, as the law requires. But the schools cannot prosper unless meetings are held as often as once a month. By frequent meetings and conversation, much valuable information may be acquired. And it would be well for committees to be continually endeavoring to obtain a knowledge of the situation of the different districts, the amount of taxable property in each district, the number of the agricultural and manufacturing population respectively, &c., &c., and this sort of information should be preserved, as it is absolutely necessary to enable them and their successors to discharge well their duties.

All acts of the school committee, to be valid, must be done at a *meeting* of the committee. Giving their assent to any measure separately, and without meeting, would be held illegal.

The manner of calling special meetings of the committee, should be regulated by by-law. If there be no by-law, the chairman should call them, and should give every member notice if possible.

Within a week after the annual town meeting, the school committee are entitled to receive from the town treasurer a report of all school moneys in his hands, specifying particularly the sources whence derived, &c.

As soon as elected, the clerk of the committee should forward to the school commissioner a list of the names of the committee, with their post-office address, and should also inform him in what way packages or bundles can most conveniently be sent to them. This will materially aid the commissioner in the discharge of the duties of his office.

Laying off Districts.—A town may vote to manage its schools collectively or by districts. If there are districts, the whole power of laying them off, making new ones, altering them, and of settling disputed boundaries, is vested by law in the school committee, subject to an appeal to the commissioner; and reasonable notice should be given in all such cases.

In laying off districts, regard should be had to the convenience of attending school, the number of scholars, the valuation of property, and ability to provide school-houses, &c. It will be always expedient to bound them by rivers, roads, or other natural or well-known boundaries, when practicable. When the lines can, without inconvenience, be so drawn as to include all of any person's farm in the same district where his dwelling-house is, it will save a great deal of trouble and expense in assessing taxes.

In New York they bound their school districts by lines running from one specified point to another, and when the line crosses any person's farm or lot, they tax the whole farm or lot in the district where the dwelling-house is, if there be one on it. But this rule is objectionable, because when a tax is contemplated, a person so situated may avoid a portion of it by a fraudulent conveyance of his land. And every purchase or sale of land so situated does practically alter the bounds of the district.

Districts must be set off by bounds including certain land. It is not sufficient, (in those towns where the schools are managed and the school-houses built by districts,) to declare that a district shall be composed of such and such *persons*. The Supreme Court of Massachusetts have declared such districts to be invalid. [7 Pick. 106, and 12 Pick. 206.]

. When a district which has built a school-house is divided, or its bounds altered so as to take off any portion of it, the joint property is to be equitably apportioned among them. If the district owe any debts, they should of course be considered in the apportionment. In

some cases this can be done by a division of the property itself. In
other cases the rent or income may be apportioned, according to the
peculiar circumstances. The school committee must decide such
cases, subject, of course, to the appeal provided by the law.

Where it is more convenient for a person belonging to one district to send to a school in another district, the school committee may
alter the bounds so as to include his house; or the trustees, or, if no
trustees, the committee may permit his children to attend such school
and pay for it under the provisions of the law. And the committee
may make the same arrangement for those who can more conveniently
attend a school situated in a neighboring town.

In every town, after the boundaries of the districts are settled, it
would be well to have a description of them *printed* for general information and circulation. This might, with propriety, be attached
to the school regulations.

The power of forming *joint* districts on the borders of the different
towns, is also confided to the school committees. Many of the manufacturing villages are on streams which are the boundaries of towns,
and are partly in both towns. In such situations the school committees should encourage the union of the adjoining districts, as both
together may be able to establish a better school, or keep one for a
longer time, or to establish them of different grades.

In assigning to a district which forms part of a joint district, its
proportion of that part of the money which is divided according to
average attendance, the committee will of course take the average
attendance of that portion of the scholars who belong to their own
town.

Location, Plans, &c.—The school committee are to locate all
school-houses, and to approve of all plans and specifications for building them. When the district is unanimous, and the location, on the
whole, unobjectional, the committee will defer to their wishes; but
in cases of dispute, they should endeavor to select such a site as will
best accommodate the greater portion of the district. Plans for the
erection and repairs of district school-houses must also be approved
by the school committee, or by the commissioner. This provision,
together with that requiring that the school committee must approve
of all rates of tuition and taxes that any district may order, was intended to operate as a salutary check against the improper exercise
of the powers given to school districts. In some districts there may
be but few legal voters; in others, the majority of voters may be
persons not interested in the property in the district; and various
other cases may happen where a minority should be protected against

abuse of taxation. And for this purpose, the law requires the approbation of the school committee, the majority of whom will probably belong to other parts of the town, and have no private or personal interest in the local controversies and disputes of the district.

For the same reason the law requires the plan of building to be appoved by the committee. The committee should therefore investigate this subject, and visit and examine the best school-houses, so as to be prepared to act when called on. They will find a variety of plans in the document on school-houses, attached to the report of the first commissioner, Hon. Henry Barnard, LL. D., which they can modify according to circustances, and from which, at least, they may derive many useful hints.

The subject of school-houses and school apparatus is most fully discussed in the work published by Mr. Barnard on school architecture, which includes all the various articles published in his different reports, while superintendent of schools in Connecticut and Rhode Island, and which cannot be too highly recommended to those wishing information on this subject.

Examining Teachers.—The examination of persons wishing to teach as principal or assistants, the granting of certificates of qualification, and the annulling of such certificates, are among the most important duties devolving on the school committee, and on their faithful performance the efficiency of the law mainly depends.

The inefficiency of the former school system in many of the towns was owing to the fact that the duties of examining teachers and visiting the schools were too generally neglected or ill performed.

The law gives the committee the power to appoint a sub-committee for the purpose of examining teachers. But it is respectfully suggested that where the whole committee can meet for this purpose it is most advisable. It will have a more imposing effect upon the teachers themselves, and incompetent persons will be less likely to present themselves.

In making such examinations, whether by the whole board, or by the sub-committee, they should inquire *first, as to moral character.* On this point, the committee should be entirely satisfied, before proceeding further. Some opinion can be formed from the general deportment and language of the applicant, but the safest course will be, with regard to those who are strangers to the committee, to insist on the written testimony of persons of the highest respectability in the towns and neighborhoods where they have resided; and especially to require the certificate of the school committee and parents where they have taught before, as to the character they have sustained, and the influence they have exerted in the school and in society.

While a committee should not endeavor to inquire into the peculiar religious or sectarian opinions of a teacher, and should not entertain any preferences or prejudices founded on any such grounds, they ought, without hesitation, to reject every person who is in the habit of ridiculing, deriding or scoffing at religion.

And while a examination should in no case be extended to the *political* opinions of the candidate, yet it may with propriety extend " to their manner in expressing such belief, or maintaining it. If that manner is in itself boisterous and disorderly, intemperate and offensive, it may well be supposed to indicate ungoverned passions, or want of sound principles of conduct, which would render its possessor obnoxious to the inhabitants of the district, and unfit for the sacred duties of a teacher of youth, who should instruct by example as well as by precept."—*N. Y. Regulations.*

Second, as to literary attainments. The lowest grade of attainments is specified in the school law, and demands a thorough knowledge of the common branches of English education. Every teacher must have been found qualified by examination, or by previous experience, which must have come to the personal knowledge of the committee, to teach the English language, arithmetic, penmanship, and the rudiments of geography and history. An examination as to the attainments of a teacher in these branches might be so conducted as to test his capacity in those particulars, to teach any grade of schools. Some reference, therefore, must be had to the condition and wants of the district schools as they now are. But no person should be considered qualified to teach any school, who cannot speak and write the English language, if not elegantly, at least correctly. He should be a good reader, and be able to make the hearer understand and feel all that the author intended. *He should be able to give the analysis as well as explain the meaning of the words of the sentence, and explain all dates, names and allusions.* He should be a good speller; and to test this, as well as his knowledge of punctuation, the use of capitals, &c., he should be required to write out his answers to some of the questions of the committee. He should understand practically the first principles of English grammar, as illustrated in his own writing and conversation. He should be able to write a good hand, to make a pen, and teach others how to do both. He should show his knowledge of geography by applying his definitions of the elementary principles to the geography of his own town, State and country, and by questions on the map and globe. He should be able to answer promptly all questions relating to the leading events of the history of the United States and his own State. In arithmetic, he should be well versed in some treaties on mental arithmetic, and be able to work out before the committee, on the blackboard or slate, such questions as will test his ability to teach the text-books on arithmetic prescribed for the class of schools he will be engaged in.

Third, his ability to instruct.—This ability includes aptness to teach, a power of simplifying difficult processes,—a skill in imparting knowledge,—of inducing pupils to try, and try in such a way that they will derive encouragement as they go along,—which must be given by nature, but may be cultivated by observation and practice. An examination into the literary qualifications of a candidate as ordinarily conducted, and even when conducted by an experienced committee man, or even by a teacher, will not always determine whether this ability is possessed, or possessed in a very eminent degree. Hence it is desirable for the committee to ascertain what success the candidate has had in other places, if he has taught before ; and if this evidence cannot be had, whether he has received any instruction in the art of teaching ; or has been educated under a successful teacher ; or has visited good schools. In conducting the examination to ascertain this point, the candidate should be asked how he would teach the several studies. He should be asked how he would proceed in teaching the alphabet to a child who had never been instructed at all in it ; as for example, whether he would give him words or single letters ; or letters having a general resemblance ; or in the order in which they are ordinarily printed ; or by copying them on a slate or blackboard, and then repeating their names after the teacher ; or by picking them out of a collection of alphabet blocks, &c., &c. So in spelling. He should be asked how he would classify his scholars in this branch, and the methods of arranging and conducting a class exercise ; how far he would adopt with the class the simultaneous method, and how far the practice of calling on each member in regular order ; how far he would put out the word to the whole class, and after requiring all to spell it *mentally*, name a particular scholar to spell it *orally ;* how far he would adopt the method of writing the word, and especially the difficult words, on a slate or blackboard ; how far he would connect spelling with the reading lessons, &c.

It will be more satisfactory sometimes, perhaps, to have a class of small scholars present at the examination, and let the candidate go through a recitation with them, so that the committee can have a practical specimen of his tact in teaching each branch of study ; in explaining and removing difficulties, &c.

The same method of examination should be carried into reading,

2

and every other branch. It is more important to know that the teacher has sound views as to methods, than that he is qualified as to literary attainments.

Fourth, ability to govern.—This is an important qualification, insisted upon by the law, and indispensable to the success of the schools. On this point the committee should call for the evidence of former experience, wherever the candidate has taught before, and when this cannot be had, the examination should elicit the plans of the teacher as to making children comfortable, keeping them all usefully employed, and interested in their studies, his best system of rewards and punishments, and examples of the kinds of punishment he would resort to in particular cases, and all other matters pertaining to the good order and government of a school. In this connection, the age, manners, bearing, knowledge of the world, love and knowledge of children, &c., of the applicant, will deserve attention.

In addition to these qualifications which the law requires, the address and personal manners and habits of the applicant should be inquired into, for these will determine in a great measure the manners and habits of the children whom he will be called upon to teach.

The most thorough and satisfactory mode of conducting the examination is by written questions and answers; it will be desirable, if the examination is conducted orally, to keep minutes of the questions and answers.

While every teacher should be found qualified in the particulars specified in the law, the certificate might show the peculiar qualification of the person to whom it is given, viz. : that he or she is peculiarly fitted for a primary school, as principal or assistant, as the case may be.

The school committee must remember that on the thoroughness and fidelity with which this duty is performed, depends in a great measure the success or failure of the school system. The whole machinery moves to bring good teachers into the schools, and to keep them as long, and under as favorable circumstances, as possible.

If the teacher adds to his other qualifications a knowledge of the art of singing, it will be an additional recommendation to him with those who desire to have a good school. Singing in school serves as a recreation and amusement, especially for the smaller scholars. It exercises and strengthens their voices and lungs, and by its influence on the disposition and morals, enables a teacher to govern his school with comparative ease.

The committee should exercise a sound discretion in the examination. If a person has been before examined by them, and the committee have often visited his school, and know him to be a good teacher, the law allows them to give him a certificate founded on this experience. But the reëxaminations can in no case do any injury, and by gradually increasing their rigor and adding to the requirements, much may be done towards raising the general standard of education. The committee should, for convenience of reference, keep a tabular list of the names of all persons examined by them, either on their common record book, or in a book kept for that purpose, with columns for the date, age, place of residence of the applicant, the result of the examination, and any other remarks that may appear worthy of remembrance.

Annulling Certificates.—As a teacher's qualifications depend not merely upon his learning, (of which a committee can judge from examination,) but upon his moral character, his disposition and temper, and his capacity to impart information, and to govern a school, in regard to all which the committee may be deceived or not fully informed ; the law gives the committee the power to annul any certificate they may have given, if on trial the teacher proves unqualified. A teacher may also refuse to adopt the proper books, may introduce improper books, may refuse to adopt what the committee deem the best methods of instruction, or may violate other regulations of the committee. In case of all annulments of certificates of teachers, the school committee, who are the only authority in the matter, must give at least five days' notice in writing of such intention, and afterwards must notify the trustee of their act.

Visitation of Schools.—There was no duty of the school committee under the old law more generally neglected than that of visitation.

The new law makes it the *express duty* of committees and trustees to visit the schools often. Without personal visits to the schools, the committee can know nothing about the teacher's capacity to impart information, or about his method of instruction and government, neither can they know the state of the register and the general conduct of the scholars.

The committee are authorized to employ some suitable person to visit the schools in their stead, and to pay him a reasonable compensation.

Visiting the schools also has the effect of encouraging the teacher in the performance of his duties ; and if the teacher is visited and treated with proper respect by the committee, trustees and parents, it materially aids to secure to him respectful treatment from the scholars, and enables him to govern his school and preserve order with ease, and without resorting to corporal punishment.

But the greatest effect is on the pupils themselves. School is now considered by many of them as a place of punishment. But if their parents and others visit them often, and take an interest in their studies and progress, it gives a new character at once to the school and the school-room, and they contemplate it with pleasure instead of dread.

It will also have the effect of accustoming the pupils to recite before strangers, and help them to get rid of that timidity and reserve which, if not early removed, may prove a serious hindrance to their success in many pursuits in after life.

While it will be advisable to assign one or more schools to each member of the committee, for the purpose of visitation and general supervision, it will be very desirable that all the schools shall be visited at least once a term by the *same* person or persons, so that a comparison can be instituted between the different teachers and schools, and the official reports and returns be made out more understandingly. The trustees and parents of each district should be invited to accompany the committee on their visits; and it will be well to encourage the teachers to visit each other's schools, with a few of their most advanced scholars.

In visiting schools, whether by the whole board, sub-committee, or individually, the following are among the objects which deserve attention:

The condition of the school-house and appurtenances; its location; size and condition of yard and out-buildings; construction, size, outward appearance, and state of repair of building; by whom built and owned, whether by town, district or proprietors; number and size of entries, and whether furnished with scraper, mat, hooks and shelves for hats, outer garments, water-pail, cup, broom, duster, etc.; dimensions of school-room, and its condition as to light, whether too much or too little,—as to the air, pure or impure,—as to temperature, whether too high or too low; modes of ventilation, whether by lowering or raising upper or lower sash, by opening into attic, by flue or otherwise; whether heated by close or open stove, fire-place or furnace; construction and arrangement of seats and desks; whether all the scholars, and especially the younger, are comfortably seated, with backs to lean against, and with their feet resting on the floor, and all facing the teacher; whether there is a platform where the teacher can overlook the whole school, and aisles to allow of his passing to every scholar, to give such instruction as may be necessary, in their seats; whether there is a place to arrange the classes for recitation, and accommodations for visitors, &c.

On entering the school, the committee will first ascertain all necessary particulars respecting the teacher, such as his certificate, general plan, &c. These will enable them to form a proper judgment of what takes place in the course of their subsequent inspection and inquiries.

The school register should be called for, and such particulars as to the number and names of the scholars, their age, parents, attendance and studies, should be gleaned, as will enable them to speak on the importance of regular and punctual attendance, to expose the evils of the contrary practice, and to commend before the whole school those who are among the most regular. An inspection of the register will inform the committee what children are not connected with the school, and a kind and timely call, a word with the parents or guardian, may save such children from ignorance, and the community from its consequences.

The committee should inquire into the number of classes, and the studies they pursue. Such exercises should be called for as will exhibit the proficiency of the pupils, and the methods of instruction adopted by the teacher, and enable the committee to judge of the tact of the teacher in imparting information. The teacher, in justice to himself and his pupils, should be allowed to conduct some of the exercises himself, and in his usual manner, as the scholars, (if not used to being visited by strangers,) will be less timid when examined by him, and the committee will have a better opportunity to see his mode of instruction. But the committee should also ask questions, and in some cases take the examination into their own hands.

It will be well to place in the hands of the more advanced scholars, written or printed questions, to be answered in writing, while the examination of other classes is going forward. And the same or similar questions should be asked in every school visited, and the answers will be to some extent an unexceptionable standard of comparison between the teachers and the schools.

The committee should be careful to notice the manner in which the pupils spell and read. In reading, especially, there is great carelessness in many of our schools. They should also observe the teacher's manners and mode of governing. If the school is not provided with proper maps, blackboards, &c., by proper remarks on their uses and importance, they may be the means of inducing the district to procure them.

Such inquiries should be made as will show how far the rules and regulations of the school committee are observed, as to teachers, books, the cleanliness and preservation of the school-house, the manners of the pupils, &c.

Great care should be taken not to wound unnecessarily the feelings of teacher or pupils, and commendation should be bestowed wherever it is deserved.

Selecting Books.—The schools have heretofore suffered much from the great variety used. It has rendered classification impossible, and whenever a scholar has changed his district or his school, a new set of books was to be purchased. Uniformity should be established in the schools of a town at least. And by proper management, by procuring some person in the town or county to act as agent, a great saving in expense to the parents can be effected. In regard to the selection, the committee are entitled to the advice of the commissioner, and the benefit of his experience; and it is expected that they in turn will coöperate with him in such measures as he may recommend or adopt to secure a uniformity of books in the State.

But no rule which a committee may adopt as to the books to be used, should be so framed or construed, as to prevent a teacher from using explanations or illustrations to be found in other books upon any particular subject. In arithmetic and algebra it will be a profitable exercise for the teacher to give the pupils occasionally for solution, questions and problems from other books besides the prescribed ones.

No book should be introduced into any public school by the committee, containing any passage or matter reflecting in the least degree upon any religious sect, or which any religious sect would be likely to consider offensive.

Rules and Regulations.—The school committee should prescribe a system of rules and regulations respecting the age, admission, attendance, classification, studies, discipline and instruction of pupils, in all the schools; the examination and duties of teachers; the kind of books to be used, &c.

The age for admission should be uniform in all the districts of a town, as otherwise some districts may have the advantage over others in the apportionment of the public money.

Apportioning Money.—The committee, having ascertained what they can depend upon from the State treasury, the town and the registry act, and having reserved an amount sufficient to defray the expense of printing their report, will apportion it as soon as possible according to law. But they are not authorized to pay out or give an order to any district which has not maintained a school for at least four months during the year preceding. The law makes a district's complying with these provisions for one year, a prerequisite to its receiving any money the next year.

As to apportioning money to a joint district, see chapter 63, section 6; and to a secondary school, supported by two districts, see chapter 63, section 4.

It will in all cases be desirable, and the safest course for the committee, to let the school money remain in the town treasury, (at interest if possible,) until the schools are kept, and not to give orders for it any faster than they are satisfied it is actually expended. It may then be paid to the teacher or his order, on his producing or sending a bill certified or allowed by the trustees, or otherwise, at the discretion of the committee.

The committee will find it greatly to their convenience to keep a separate book for their accounts. In this book a separate account might be opened with each school or school district, in which the district should be from time to time credited with the money apportioned to them, and then charged with the orders which have been given to them.

Another separate account may be so kept, by listing all the sums of money appropriated to schools on one side, and all orders given on the other, as to show at any time the balance under the committee's control.

Reports.—By chapter 65, section 5, trustees are to report to the school committee, at such time and in such form as the committee or commissioner may prescribe. These returns must be made in season to enable the committee to digest them, and prepare a report to the commissioner by July 1st; for which reports the commissioner will furnish forms. The committee are, also, at the annual town meeting, to make a written or printed report to the town, of all their doings, the condition of the schools, plans for their improvement, &c.

The committee are authorized to reserve enough (not exceeding $20) out of the school money to print their reports. And it is believed that no part of the school expenditure would do more good and tend more to keep up an interest in the schools, than this.

The committee must aid in organizing districts, by giving the notice for the first meeting. And when there are no trustees, or when the trustees neglect to call meetings, the committee must call them. In such cases they may direct the mode of notice.

Any district when met, may vote to devolve upon the committee, with their consent, the whole management of their schools; and in that case the committee can exercise in that district all the powers which the district itself might exercise, may keep the school, have the custody of the school-house, fix the rate of tuition, &c.

If any district neglect to organize, or if organized, shall, for the

space of six months neglect or refuse to establish a school, the committee may, either by themselves or their agent, employ and pay a
teacher for the district.

Gradation of Schools.—The school committee can promote a gradation of schools, or a separation of the younger and the older scholars,
and the primary and advanced studies into distinct schools or departments.   But it has been decided that they cannot compel a district to
establish graded schools.

Whenever the schools of a town are managed independent of
districts, a sufficient number of schools of different grades can be
established by the committee, at convenient locations, varying in the
studies pursued according to the circumstances of the population.

And in towns which are divided into districts, there are many
villages and thickly settled districts, where a gradation of schools can
be introduced. By separating the small children from the older
scholars, the instruction of both can be carried on to greater advantage, and with a great economy of time and expense. By putting
the small children under the care of a female teacher, they can have
more of the teacher's time devoted to them, and will learn with
a rapidity surprising to those who have not seen the effect of it. This
enables the teacher of the large scholars to devote his whole attention
to their improvement.

They may recommend the union of two or more adjacent districts,
for the purpose of establishing a secondary or grammar school for the
older and more advanced pupils of each district. This can be done
to advantage in almost every town.

Records.—At the beginning of the year the committee should have
a warrant or certificate of their election from the town clerk, (see
form,) which it would be well to have made upon the record book
itself, as loose papers are often lost. Then let the certificate of
engagement follow in order.

The clerk should record any motion negatived, as well as those
adopted, as parties may be interested, and have a right to appeal, in
many cases, from a negative vote as well as from an affirmative one.

When it can be conveniently done, the minutes of the proceedings,
as drawn out by the clerk, should be read in open meeting, or at the
next meeting, for correction, if necessary. Misunderstandings may
thus be prevented.

The clerk should always record the names of the members of the
committee present at any meeting. He should also keep the copies
of all abstracts, and all reports made to the commissioner, so that the
committee may have them for future reference and comparison.

TRUSTEES.

One or three trustees are to be appointed by a district at its annual meeting. If by any accident an election is not made then, or if a vacancy occurs, the district may elect afterwards. And if a special meeting is called to fill a vacancy occasioned by resignation, the warrant to call the meeting must state that an election is to be held. Trustees hold their offices until their successors are appointed; and can only be removed from their office for cause, and after notice and trial.

If there are three trustees, a majority can act. "Where a body or board of officers is constituted by law to perform a trust for the public, or to execute a power or perform a duty prescribed by law, it is not necessary that all should concur in the act done. The act of the majority is the act of the body. And where all have due notice of the time and place of meeting in the manner prescribed by law, if so prescribed,—or by the rules and regulations of the body itself, if there be any,—otherwise if reasonable notice is given, and no practice or unfair means are used to prevent all from attending and participating in the proceeding, it is no objection that all the members do not attend, if there be a quorum." [21 Pick. Rep. 28.] All business must be done at a meeting of the board.

The trustees must employ the teacher. In employing a teacher or assistant teacher, trustees should be cautious to employ no one who has not a legal certificate, and not to employ one after notice that his certificate is annulled, as in such a case the trustees would be held personally liable for the teacher's wages. (See the form.) The trustees should see that the teacher keeps a proper register of attendance, in order that his district may receive its due portion of school money next year; and when the school is over, this register should be deposited with the trustees, or in the office of the clerk of the district. They should require the teacher to furnish them with such items of information as are necessary to make out their annual report to the town committee, which report should be made about the first of May, or sooner if the school is out, or at such time as the committee shall fix. Forms for these reports will be furnished to the districts, and can be obtained from the committee or from the town clerk's office.

If trustees appropriate any of the public money to pay a teacher not legally examined, they are liable to a penalty.

The school must be kept four months in order to obtain the money for the next year. And the trustees, without waiting for a vote of the district, may, if the public money is insufficient, assess a rate sufficient to keep the school four months, taking care, however, to have the rate approved by the school committee, and exempting those they consider unable to pay.

If any scholars can more conveniently attend school in an adjoining district, trustees are authorized to make a bargain for that purpose. They should also take care that the school is kept in a house which will not be disapproved of by the committee of the town.

Trustees should regard the visiting of the schools as one of the most important of their duties, and which should by no means be neglected.

When a district is organized and has trustees, they are to notify the annual and special district meetings, and if there be no district school-house, or place appointed by the district, they are to fix the place of meeting. If the trustees on application neglect to call a meeting, the school committee may call it.

Trustees, for refusal to discharge any duty, call a meeting, assess a tax, &c., &c., are liable to a penalty. And the supreme court would probably, upon application, compel any school officer, by writ of mandamus, to discharge any duty plainly imposed on him by the law.

Trustees should encourage meetings of teachers in their neighborhoods, for mutual improvement. And if any teacher neglects or refuses to attend a teachers' institute, when organized under proper auspices, and when he conveniently can, it should be regarded as a sign of unfitness for the place. No one is so well qualified, as not to be able to learn from his fellows many useful hints as to methods of teaching, books, &c., and no one should be unwilling or too proud to learn.

Trustees should see that an inventory of all the maps, books and other property belonging to the district, is made from time to time, and preserved among the papers of the district.

Every district should possess a dictionary, to be kept as an appendage to the school-house. Maps of the State, the United States, and of the town (if there is one,) should be procured.

The trustees should keep a regular account of all moneys they may receive from assessments or other sources.

Trustees should recollect that in order to obtain from the school committee any order for money, they must have made a proper return from their district, for the year ending on the first of May previous, and must also furnish to the committee a certificate that the " teachers' money," (that is, the money which the district received from the town treasurer as their part of the State appropriation,) for the year ending the first of May previous, had been applied to the wages of teachers, and for no other purpose whatever.

The return of the district should include the whole time during which any portion of the public money has been used to support the school.

For further particulars, see the law. See also the forms.

DISTRICTS.

In order to be eligible to any district office, a person must possess the qualifications of a voter; and any voter may be elected to any district office.

It is sufficient if the person elected have the qualifications of a voter at the time of his election. He will not afterwards lose the office by losing his qualification to vote.

To enable a person to vote in district meeting, he must reside in the district and possess the qualifications requisite to entitle him to have his name put upon the voting list of the town; but his name need not actually be upon the list.

Meetings.—As to notifying meetings, see chap. 62, sec. 6. When met, the district must organize by choosing a moderator and clerk. The moderator need not be engaged. The clerk may be engaged in open meeting by the moderator, and the clerk may then engage all other district officers, and his record will be evidence of his own and their engagements. Every district meeting may choose a moderator, who will preside at the meeting and any adjournments of it. But the clerk is an annual officer. When met they may vote to devolve the care of the district school on the school committee, or may appoint one or three trustees to manage it. If they fail to appoint officers at their annual meeting, they may appoint them afterwards, and may fill vacancies at any time.

If the moderator refuses to put questions to vote, or he or any other district officer violates the law, he is liable to pay a fine.

The annual district meeting is to be in March, April or May, but special meetings may be called by the trustees at any time.

Inhabitants of districts may be witnesses in all cases, and so may prove (if disputed) the legality of the notice and meeting, and the clerk's record that the meeting has been duly notified, will be *prima facie* evidence of the fact.

Vacancies may happen from a variety of causes. A resignation need not be in writing. The person resigning should give information of it to the person or corporation authorized to fill the vacancy.

At all district meetings a reasonable time should be allowed for the people to assemble. And if in the course of proceeding, any legal vote is rejected, or any illegal vote is received by the moderator, by which the result is affected, an appeal may be taken to the commissioner for redress.

Districts may fix a rate of tuition to be paid by the parents towards the support of the school, (provided said rate be approved by the school committee.) But no scholar can be excluded from the school on account of the inability of his parents to pay the rate.

Or, the district may authorize the trustees to fix the rate or assessment. And either district or trustees must exempt such as they consider unable to pay the assessment. And to guard against any abuse of this power, if a person is assessed for a rate who is unable to pay, he may apply to any justice of the peace and be discharged on taking the poor debtor's oath, without waiting to be committed to jail. A liberal discretion should be used in exempting poor parents from the rate. Few will claim an exemption in such a case unless there is real inability.

Quorum of District Meetings.—It has been repeatedly decided in the courts of England and this country, that at common law, where there is no statute provision, when a meeting of a corporation, consisting of an *indefinite* number of persons, (as towns, districts, &c.,) is properly notified, no particular number is requisite to form a quorum, but a majority of those present may act.

To require a majority of the voters of the district, would in many cases prevent the doing of any business at all. And to fix any particular number would be difficult, because there are some districts where this number would be more than the whole number of voters. The law has therefore required the notice of the meeting to be given with great particularity, and then presumes that every voter who does not attend, assents to what is done by those present.

At the same time, it will not be advisable to proceed in any matter of importance, such as laying a tax, &c., unless a respectable number of voters attend.

Reconsideration.—A district may reconsider and rescind any vote at any time before any contract has been made under it. But after a contract has been made, or an individual has incurred any expense or liabilities in consequence of a vote of the district, they cannot with justice rescind it. And if rescinded, they will be held liable to make good all damages and losses incurred.

Taxation.—The districts have power to purchase, hire and repair school-houses, provide blackboards, maps, furniture, a clock or timepiece, a school library, bell, record and account-books, mats, scrapers, water-pails, and other necessary and useful appendages. The law gives them a general power to tax for school purposes. They may tax to pay rent of a hired house. They may also tax to repair a hired house, provided they have a valid lease of it for a definite period. And to guard against any abuse of this power, the tax must be approved by the school committee, and the plans for building and repairs must also be approved by the committee or commissioner. And in all cases of laying taxes, it would be better to specify the precise amount, or the precise rate of the tax.

Money to pay for fuel and tuition may be raised either by a tax on the property of the district or by an assessment on the parents of the scholars. But an assessment for this purpose must be authorized by the district, except that the trustees are authorized to raise a rate sufficient to keep a four months' school. And the votes must in all cases be approved by the school committee.

[See the forms and notes, and especially the notes to the form of a vote for laying a tax.]

Use of school-house for other purposes.—A school-house built or bought by taxation on the property of the district, should not be used for any other purpose than keeping a school, or for purposes directly connected with education, except by the general consent of the tax-paying voters. The law gives the district the power of raising money by tax for no other purposes. To construe it otherwise, would be indirectly to give to the majority of a district the power to erect a meeting-house for themselves, and to tax those of a different persuasion, who constituted the minority, to help build it. But where a school-house is given to the district or built by subscription, its use will of course depend upon the terms of the donation or subscription.

A district cannot vote to dissolve itself. Such a vote will be wholly null and void. It can be dissolved by the school committee alone.

UNION OF DISTRICTS.

There are three provisions made in the law for uniting districts. Any two districts may form a partial union for the purpose of supporting a higher, secondary or grammar school. This would not probably be found so convenient in practice as an entire union under the succeeding provisions.

Any contiguous districts in adjoining towns may be united by the school committees, and adjoining districts in the same town may consolidate themselves. When united they constitute a single district, and their affairs must be managed in the same way as if originally one district. They may prescribe the mode of notifying their meetings, lay taxes, &c. But they will be entitled to the same proportion of public money they would receive if not united.

DISTRICT CLERK.

The district clerk should be engaged by the moderator in open meeting and make a record of it. If not engaged in open meeting, he should be engaged before some officer mentioned in chap. 71, sec. 2, and have a certificate of it, which it would be better to have made in the district record book. When engaged, he may engage all other district officers, and should enter all such cases in his record book.

He should make himself thoroughly acquainted with all the provisions of the law relating to district meetings, notices, &c., as upon his proceedings and proper management their legality will in many cases depend.

When a trustee, treasurer, &c., is elected, the clerk should make out and sign and seal a warrant or certificate of his election, upon which he may be engaged. [See forms.]

The clerk should, at the request of any person interested, record a motion which is negatived, as well as a motion passed as in many cases a person may be entitled to an appeal. And he should record the number and names of the voters on request.

In the record of every meeting, it would be well for the clerk to state how the meeting was notified, and when and by whom the notices were posted up. In many cases at some distance of time, it might be important to know how the meeting was notified, and the evidence of it should not be left to depend upon mere recollection. The record of the clerk is made *prima facie* evidence that the meeting was legally notified, and inhabitants of the district can be admitted to prove the notice. But it would be easy and best to preserve one of the original notices themselves, especially when a tax is to be voted.

It would be well also for the clerk, at the close of every meeting, to read aloud the minutes he has made of the proceedings, so that any mistake may be corrected at the time.

The clerk is to procure a bound record book at the expense of the district. For any wilful neglect or refusal to perform any duty, he is liable to indictment, and the supreme court would probably, upon application, compel him by writ of mandamus to perform any duty. [See *Clerk*, in the Index.]

DISTRICT TREASURER.

It would be well for the treasurer to have a certificate of his election or warrant [see form] and be engaged. He need not give bond unless required. But if the district requires him to give bond, the district should fix the sum and approve of the surety or sureties.

His duties are very simple : to keep the district's money, if they have any, pay it out to order, and keep proper accounts of it, and exhibit them to the trustees or district when required.

DISTRICT COLLECTOR.

[*See the forms for collecting taxes and notes.*] If the district requires the collector to give bond, the district should fix the sum. And it would be well also to have the district approve of the surety or sureties.

TEACHERS.

Every teacher is required to keep a register of all the scholars attending the school, their sex, names, ages, names of parents or guardians, the time when they enter and leave school, their daily attendance, and the dates when the school is visited by the commissioner, committee or trustees. Forms for these registers will be prepared by the commissioner. He must also furnish the trustees or district with such information as may be necessary to make the returns required by the school committee.

The teacher should inform the committee of the time of commencing and closing his school, in order that they may know when to visit it.

It is important that the register be correctly kept, and the average rightly calculated, as upon that depends the amount of money the district will receive next year.

To ascertain the average, place the number of those who have attended each half day in a column under each other successively, add together, and divide the sum by the number of half days the school has been kept. The result will be the average to be reported. In case the school is kept longer than the four months required by law, the committee must use their discretion in fixing a rule for calculating the average. It should be uniform in each town. Where a summer term and a winter term are kept, and a different set of scholars attend each term, the following will probably answer : Calculate the average for the first term of four months, as before stated. Then for the other term take the names of all those who did not attend the other term, calculate the average of their attendance and add it to the first.

A uniform rule should be adopted as to scholars belonging to one district who attend school in another.

When a district allows any of the children belonging to it to attend school in another district, and pays for them, it seems reasonable that the district which pays for them should be entitled to reckon them in making out its own average attendance.

The teacher should conform to all regulations of the school committee, in regard to hours, discipline, books, etc., as for any violation of them his certificate may be annulled, or he may be dismissed. He may, (if the school committee by regulation authorize it,) suspend a scholar temporarily, until a hearing can be had before the committee, in which case he should immediately notify the committee.

The teacher should assist the trustees by all the means in his power, in making proper reports, as upon the accuracy and fulness of these reports may depend the success or failure of many provisions of the law, as well as the wisdom of future alterations of it.

The law requires that the teacher should be qualified to teach certain branches. But he may teach other branches, and should endeavor to qualify himself for teaching the higher branches.

If the teacher has a proper sense of the importance of his position, and conducts himself accordingly, he will secure to himself the affection and respect of the people of his district, by exerting his utmost powers to promote the moral and intellectual advancement, not only of his scholars, but of the community around him. The moral influence he may exert by his example and instructions, can hardly be estimated. And he may, by encouraging lectures and literary meetings, aid in diffusing much useful information.

In regard to the use of the Bible in schools, two observations occur here. If the committee prescribe, or the teacher wishes to have the Bible read in school, it should not be forced upon any children whose parents have any objections whatever to its use. In most cases the teacher will have no difficulty with the parents on this subject, if he conducts with proper kindness and courtesy. In the next place, no scholars should be set to read in the Bible at school, until they have learned to read with tolerable fluency. To use it as a text-book for the younger scholars, often has the effect of leading them to look upon it with the same sort of careless disregard, and sometimes dislike, with which they regard their other school-books, instead of that respect and veneration with which this book of books should always be treated and spoken of.

There is another object, in the attainment of which teachers may materially aid. In almost every school, there will be pupils studying surveying. By encouraging these to survey the limits of the district, he may not only give his scholars most valuable lessons in the practice of the art, but by overseeing and ascertaining its correctness, may aid in procuring a good map of the town and State. These maps might be drawn on a scale of   rods to an inch, and represent the rivers, roads, principal buildings and farms, and any remarkable monuments and natural features of the district. Copies could be sent to the school committee, who might put them together, and thus obtain a correct map of their township.

Power to Punish.—The teacher should endeavor to exercise an inspection over the conduct of his scholars at all times. But the power to punish for offences committed out of school is doubtful.

In a case where a boy had committed a theft out of school, the teacher called him to account for it, and punished him for refusing to answer. The court ruled that the teacher had no right to punish him for refusing to confess a crime for which he might be punished at law.

It has always been difficult to define the extent of the power of the teacher over his pupils out of school. The same difficulty has been met with in other states and countries.

The following upon this subject is from an excellent French treatise upon education, by J. Willm, Inspector of the Academy at Strasbourg, (p. 176) :

"The last question which presents itself is, how far teachers should pay attention to the conduct of pupils out of school, and especially at the time when they resort to it or return home. The road leading to school is truly a part of it, if we may so speak, as well as the play-ground. Consequently any disorders committed by the pupils on it, ought to be suppressed by the teacher. He ought especially to watch over them at their play, for the sake of discipline, as well as for that of education in general. Their games are, as has been said, of serious importance to him. The conduct of the pupils, when under the paternal roof, and everywhere but in the school or the road leading to it, escapes all the means of discipline; but the teacher ought not to be indifferent to that conduct, especially in the country ; he should carefully inquire concerning it, for the sake of moral education. For the same reason, he will have to watch over his own conduct out of school, and avoid whatever might tend to diminish the respect his pupils owe to him, and which is the chief condition of the success of his mission."

The following remarks upon the same subject are from the tenth report of Hon. Horace Mann, late secretary of the Board of Education in Massachusetts:

"The question is not without some practical difficulty, how far the school committee and teachers may exercise authority over school children, before the hour when the school begins, or after the hour when it closes, or outside of the school-house door or yard.

"On the one hand, there is certainly some limit to the jurisdiction of the committee and teachers, out of school hours and out of the school-house ; and on the other hand, it is equally plain if their jurisdiction does not commence until the minute for opening the school has arrived, nor until the pupil has passed within the door of the school-room, that all the authority left to them in regard to some of the most sacred objects for which our schools were instituted, would be but of little avail. To what purpose would the teacher prohibit profane or obscene language among his scholars, within the school-room and during school hours, if they could indulge it with impunity, and to any extent of wantonness, as soon as the hour for dismissing the school should arrive ? To what purpose would he forbid quarrelling and fighting among the scholars, at recess, if they could engage in single combat, or marshal themselves into hostile parties for a general encounter within the precincts of the school-house, within the next five minutes after the school-house should be closed ? And to what purpose would he repress insolence to himself, if a scholar, as soon as he had passed the threshold, might shake his fist in his teacher's face, and challenge him to personal combat ?

"These considerations would seem to show that there must be a portion of time, both before the school commences and after it has closed, and also a portion of space between the door of the school-house and that of the paternal mansion, where the jurisdiction of the parent on one side, and of the committee and teachers on the other, is concurrent.

"Many of the school committees in this commonwealth have acted in accordance with these views, and have framed regulations for the government of the scholars, both before and after school hours, and while going to and returning from the school. The same principle of necessity, by virtue of which this jurisdiction, out of school hours, and beyond school premises, is claimed, defines its extent and affixes its limit. It is claimed because the great objects of discipline and of moral culture would be frustrated without it. When not essential, therefore, to the attainment of these objects, it should be forborne."

That the teacher may know that the law has amply provided for the protection of his school against all who may be disposed to disturb it, we publish here the provision of the law:

"Every person who shall be convicted of wilfully interrupting or disturbing any town or ward meeting, any assembly of people met for religious worship, or any public or private school, or any meeting lawfully and peaceably held for purposes of literary or scientific improvement, either within or without the place where such meeting or school is held, shall be imprisoned not exceeding one year, or fined not exceeding five hundred dollars."

A complaint for this offence may be made to the attorney-general, or any justice of the peace.

APPEALS.

The law has wisely provided a cheap and efficient mode of settling all disputes arising under the school law. It was intended to save the expense of litigation to districts and individuals, and it is believed that it has already had the effect of saving a great expenditure of money in this way, as well as effecting a more speedy settlement of difficulties, which, if continued, would interrupt the harmony of the districts and injure the schools. An appeal may be taken to the commissioner, [see the Forms,] and he will hear the parties without cost, and his decision is to be final. When questions of law arise, provision is made for laying them before one of the judges of the supreme court, but the judges will not examine or hear the parties upon the facts of the case.

Any party neglecting to appeal from a vote to tax, or assessment of a tax, cannot question it afterwards, provided the meeting was legally notified, and the tax approved, &c.

It has been settled that an appeal brings the whole question up, and that the commissioner in many cases is not confined to confirming or reversing the proceedings appealed from, but may make a new decision.

All appeals, however, should be taken within a reasonable time, and before any contract is made, or liability incurred, under the vote or act appealed from. If the appeal is not made within such a reasonable time, that circumstance alone will be a sufficient reason for dismissing it. And no appeal will be entertained unless made by the party aggrieved.

DEAF, DUMB, BLIND, IDIOTS, AND INSANE.

The sum appropriated for the deaf and dumb, blind and idiots, is two thousand five hundred dollars annually, and the governor of the State is appointed to distribute it.

As there are a number of these in every town in the State, the school committees and friends of education and humanity should look them up and see that they receive their proper share of the appropriations.

LIBRARIES.

Towns and districts are authorized to maintain school libraries. In the greater part of the towns library associations have been formed, and in some towns, several. These school libraries alone, now contain a great number of volumes, accessible to all. In all towns or neighborhoods where there are none, exertions should be made at once to obtain them. The commissioner will always be ready to aid in every way in his power.

A list of the school libraries already formed, may be seen in the Journal, vol. 3, p. 428. For many of these the public are indebted to the exertions of the first commissioner, Mr. Barnard, aided by several public-spirited gentlemen in Providence.

The following is the proper form for the constitution of an association for establishing and maintaining a public library:

FORM OF INCORPORATION.

We, the subscribers, agree to associate and incorporate ourselves for the purpose of maintaining a public library, by the name of the   under the provisions contained for that purpose in the Revised Statutes, passed at the January session of the general assembly, A. D. 1857, and to be governed by the following constitution:

ARTICLE 1. This association shall be called the   . The library shall be established and maintained at such place or places within the town of   as the directors may from time to time appoint.

2. The officers of the association shall be a president, vice president, secretary, treasurer, and librarian, who shall constitute a board of directors for the management of the business of the association, according to such rules as the association may from time to time adopt.

3. The annual meeting shall be held at   on   and any officer shall be elected by ballot if demanded by any   members. [The treasurer and librarian shall give bonds to the corporation in the sum of   each, with security to the satisfaction of the president for the faithful discharge of their duties.]

4. Any member, for disorderly or immoral conduct, may be expelled, and any officer, for misconduct, may be removed at any regularly notified meeting of the society.

5. The directors may make all such regulations as they may deem proper for the government of the library, and prescribe fines for non-compliance, and may, in any case of misuse of books, prohibit any person from using the library until satisfaction is made.

6. The library shall be held by the association, not in shares for the benefit of shareholders, but in trust for the public benefit; to be open to all who shall comply with such reasonable rules as shall from time to time be made by the association or directors; and for the purpose of continuing the existence of the corporation, the association will from time to time elect as members such persons as they shall think most likely to coöperate zealously in promoting its objects. No member shall be admitted unless proposed at a previous meeting.

[NOTE TO ART. 6.—This section will answer for all cases where the library is established by donations, and is intended to be for the benefit of the whole public. And this is undoubtedly the best plan for getting up such libraries. In this case, the corporation might be named "The Trustees of the   Library."

But if the library is intended to be owned in shares, and for the benefit of the shareholders, this article should be altered accordingly. They will then have the power to assess the shares and to sell them for non-payment of assessments. In this case, the shareholders will be the members and compose the corporation. The law provides how the shares may be transferred.]

7. This constitution may be amended at any annual meeting, provided notice of the intended amendment has been given at some previous meeting. The secretary shall cause this constitution and all alterations thereof to be recorded in the records of land evidence of the town of   as the law requires.

The above are all the provisions necessary to be inserted in the constitution.   All other provisions had better be made in the shape of rules or regulations, which might be altered from time to time with less trouble.

Whenever it is intended to establish a permanent library, it will always be most prudent to be incorporated as above.   If a library is owned by several persons unincorporated, it will be liable to division, and each one's interest liable to attachment.   In a corporation, the share only could be attached, and where the corporation hold the library merely as trustees, (as provided in Art. 6, above,) no individual would have any attachable interest whatever.

FORMS.

These forms have been drawn out in order to assist those who may be disposed to undertake any office or duty under the school laws, to save them expense and trouble, and to bring about a uniformity of practice, as far as can be done. These forms are not prescribed by law, but are believed to conform substantially to the law, and to be safe precedents.

1. Warrant or Certificate of Election of School Officers.

To   of   greeting:

This certifies that you, the said   were at a [town or district] meeting, held on the   day of   A. D. 18   chosen to the office of   of [the town or district No.   ] and are by virtue of said appointment fully authorized and empowered to discharge all the duties of said office, and to exercise all the powers thereto belonging, according to law.

[l. s.] Witness my hand, and the seal of said [town or district] hereto affixed by me, this   day of   A. D. 18

---

2. Engagement of School Officers.

Town of   A. D. 18

Before the subscriber personally appeared   and took an oath to support the constitution of the United States, the constitution and laws of this State, and faithfully to discharge the duties of the office of school committee [or clerk, trustee, treasurer of school district No.   as the case may be] so long as he continues therein.

A B, Justice of the Peace,
        or Notary, as the case may be.

32 FORMS.

3. *Certificate to a Teacher from a Committee.*

The school committee of the town of   hereby certify that
A B, of   is qualified to teach in the public schools in said town,
according to the provisions of the acts relating to public schools.
This certificate is to be valid within said town for one year from the
date thereof, unless previously annulled by the school committee or
some superior authority.

In behalf of the school committee of said town.

Date.   Chairman or Clerk.

---

4. *Form for Annulling a Certificate.*

To the trustees of school districts in the town of   and all others
it may concern :

Whereas, the school committee of this town did, on the   · day
of   A. D. 18   issue to   of   a certificate of qualification as
a teacher in the public schools : Now know ye, that upon further
examination, investigation and trial, the said   has been found
deficient and unqualified, [or the said   has refused to conform to
the regulations made by the committee, as the case may be,] and we
do therefore, by the authority given us by law, declare the said certificate to be annulled and void from this date, of which all persons
whose duty it is to employ teachers of public schools, are hereby
requested to take notice.

By order and in behalf of the school commitee of the town of

Date.   Chairman or Clerk.

Note.—If a complaint is made against a teacher, it will be imperative that he
shall be notified before a decision on his case. And notice of the annulling should
be immediately given to the trustees of the district, and generally, in order to prevent his being again employed.

---

5. *Memorandum of a Contract with a Teacher.*

This agreement, made this   day of   A. D. 18   between
A B, &c., [trustee, school committee or agent appointed by the
school committee, as the case may be,] of   on the one part, and
X Y, of   on the other part, witnesses, that the said X Y hereby
agrees to teach, for the compensation herein mentioned, a district
school in and for said district, at   [specify the building, if desired,]

for the term of   months' [or weeks] commencing   and ending
      and the said X Y further engages to exert the utmost of his ability in conducting said school, and improving the education and morals of the scholars; to keep such registers and make such returns to the trustees and to the school committee as may be required of him, and in all respects to conform to all such regulations for the government of said school as may be made by the school committee of said town, and to the provisions of the laws regulating public schools. And in case the certificate of qualification of said X Y should be annulled, or if he shall not keep the register and make return, as aforesaid, or should violate such regulations as aforesaid, this agreement from thenceforth shall be of no effect. And the said [committee, trustee, or agent] agree to pay the said X Y therefor at the rate of   per month, [or per week] to be paid at the end of each month [or the term] out of the school money by law apportioned to said district, and the legal assessments which may be made, and in no event out of the private property of the contractor. And it is further agreed, that the possession of the school-house and its appurtenances shall at all times be considered as being in the trustees [or school committee or agent.]

[L. S.] Witness our hands and seals hereto, the day first   above mentioned.

 Sealed and executed in presence of

---

6. *Notice of the First Meeting of a District.*

 Notice is hereby given that there will be a meeting of the legal voters of School District No.   in the town of   at the school-house in said district, [if no school-house, then the school committee must appoint a place] at   o'clock in the   noon, on   the   day of   A. D. 18   for the purpose of organizing said district, of electing officers for said district for the ensuing year, or for the purpose of considering the expediency of building [or repairing] the school-house in said district, and laying a tax on the ratable property of the district therefor, [as the case may be] and of transacting any other business which may lawfully come before said meeting.

 By order and in behalf of the school committee of said town.

 Date.   Chairman, or Clerk.

5

7.　*Notice of Annual District Meeting.*

Notice is hereby given to the legal voters of School District No. of the town of　　that the annual meeting of said district, for the choice of officers and the transaction of any other business which may lawfully come before said meeting, will be held on　　the　　day of　　of　　A. D. 18　at　　o'clock in the　　noon, at

Date.　　　　　　　　　　　　　　　　Trustee or Trustees.

Note.—A special meeting may be called by like form, except that the *object* of all special meetings must be stated.

8.　*Application to Trustees for a Special Meeting.*

To A B, &c., trustee or trustees of School District No.

The subscribers respectfully request that you would call a meeting of the legal voters of School District No.　　as soon as the legal notice therefor can conveniently be given, for the purpose of fixing the rate of tuition to be paid by the parents, guardians or employers of children attending school—of taking measures to establish a school library—of considering the propriety of building, repairing or removing a district school-house—or of raising money by a tax on the ratable estates of the district for the purpose of, &c., [as the case may be.]

　　　　　　　　To be signed by at least five persons qualified to vote.
　Date.

9.　*Commencement of District Records.*

For first meeting.—At a meeting of the legal voters of School District No.　　of the town of　　called by the school committee of said town, and notified according to law, [here in some cases it may be advisable to state particularly now the notice was given,] and held according to notice at the district school-house, on the　　day of A. D. 18　at　　o'clock in the　　noon.

For annual meeting.—At the annual meeting of the legal voters of School District No. of the town of notified by the trustees of said district according to law, [in some cases specify as above,] and held according to notice at the district school-house, [or as may be] on the day of A. D. 18 at o'clock in the noon.

For special meeting.—At a meeting of the legal voters of School District No. of the town of held (in pursuance of an an application to the trustees) at on and which meeting was duly notified by the trustees as the law requires.

For adjourned meeting.—At a meeting of the legal voters of School District No. of the town of held according to adjournment, at on

10. *Form for Choosing Officers, &c.*

The following named persons were chosen to the offices set against their respective names, viz.:

  C D, Clerk, &c.   , A B, Moderator.

Or, instead of above, say—

Voted, that A B, be appointed moderator of this meeting.

Voted, that C D, be appointed clerk, [or trustee, treasurer, &c.,] of this district, [in place of O P, resigned, &c., if such be the case,] to hold his office until the next annual meeting, and until his successor is appointed.

The clerk then, in presence of the meeting, took the oath in the form prescribed in chapter 71, section 2, of the Revised Statutes, administered by E F, Esq., justice of the peace, or [public notary, moderator, senator, judge, or town clerk.]

It was moved by A B, and seconded by C D, that and after discussion the question was put and the motion was rejected, or adopted.

Voted, that the trustee [or trustees] of the district be authorized to fix such a rate of tuition or assessment, for the purpose of supporting the public school in this district, the ensuing year, as they may deem necessary, subject to the conditions of chapter 61, sections 3 and 4.

11. *Vote of a District, prescribing Mode of Notifying Meetings.*

Whereas, each school district has by law the power to prescribe the *manner* of notifying all future district meetings,—

Voted, that hereafter all such meetings shall be notified by posting up the notices signed by the proper officers and for the time specified by law, at the following places within this district, namely, on the sign-post of the tavern, now occupied by A B, on the door of the school-house, court-house, grist-mill, or in some conspicuous place in the shop or store now kept by L M, &c., [as the district may decide.]

NOTE.—Experience shows that notices put up in the inside of a house, in a bar-room, shop, &c., are very seldom attended to, especially if they be in writing, not printed. A sign-post, a large tree, close by the travelled part of the road, the railing of a bridge, the outside of a door, &c., are the places where they would be most likely to be seen. In some cases where there is a mill, store, &c., *out* of the district, to which the people of the district often resort, it would be well to put up a notice there, in addition to the notices within the district.

But the power to prescribe the mode of notice does not authorize a district to dispense with notice, or to prescribe a less number of days than five.

12. *Vote of District to devolve care of School on School Committee.*

Voted, (if the school committee of this town consent thereto and accept thereof,) that all the powers and duties of this district, and the trustees thereof, relating to keeping public schools in this district be, and they are hereby devolved on said school committee, until this district shall choose a new trustee or trustees, or shall otherwise legally direct.

NOTE.—A copy of this vote, with a proper heading, "At a meeting of," &c., attested by the clerk, should be furnished to the committee.

13. *Vote of District to Build School-house.*

Voted, that a school-house be erected at or upon   for the use of the public schools in this district, and that   be a committee to cause the same to be erected, the said committee first procuring the plans and specifications for the building, to be approved by the commissioner of public schools, or by the committee of the town, according to law, and that the said   shall have full power, in the name and behalf of the district, to sign, seal and execute any contracts which may be necessary to carry out this vote, to superintend the execution of said contracts, and to do any other matter or thing which may be necessary to carry out this vote.

NOTE.—The location, (unless before made,) must be made by the school committee.

14. *Form of a Contract to Build School-house.*

Articles of agreement made and executed on the   day of
A. D. 18   between A B, of   on the one part, and School
District No.   of the town of   county of   State of
on the other part.

The said A B, for himself, his heirs, executors and administrators, doth hereby covenant and agree with the school district and their assigns, that he, the said A B, his heirs, executors and administrators, for the considerations herein expressed, shall, and will, within the space of   months from the date hereof, erect, build, and completely cover over and finish upon, [here describe the lot,] and upon such spot in said lot as said school district or their proper officers may direct, a house, out-buildings and fences, for the purpose of a district school-house and appendages, according to plans, elevation and specification more particularly expressed in a schedule hereto attached and signed by said parties, and which is hereby made part and parcel of this agreement; and also shall and will perform and execute all the works mentioned in the said schedule, and in the manner therein mentioned, and within the time aforesaid; and also shall and will furnish and provide at his own charge, good and sufficient materials of the sorts and quality expressed in said schedule, and all such other materials as may be necessary for the erecting and fully completing the house, out-houses and fences aforesaid, according to the plans and specifications aforesaid.

And it is further agreed between said parties, that if the said A B, his heirs, executors or administrators, shall not within the space of time above mentioned finish and complete all said works as aforesaid, then said school district, or their agent, may go on and complete said works, at the cost and charge of the said A B, his heirs, executors and administrators, and may deduct the same from the compensation herein agreed to be paid for said buildings and works; and the said A B, his heirs, executors and administrators, shall also be liable for any other damages incurred by said district by said failure, and shall also be liable to said district for any damages incurred by any other unreasonable delay in completing the works aforesaid.

And the said school district doth hereby covenant and agree with the said A B, his heirs, executors, administrators and assigns, that upon the completion of said works as aforesaid, the said school district shall and will pay to the said A B, his executors, administrators or assigns, on or before the   day of   A. D. 18   the sum of dollars, as full compensation for his services in building and completing said works.

And it is further agreed, that if said school district or their agents shall direct any any more work to be done upon or around said buildings than is hereinbefore agreed, the said district shall pay the expense thereof, in addition to the compensation aforesaid. And if said district, or their agents shall direct to omit or diminish any part of the work hereinbefore agreed to be done and expressed in said schedule, then there shall be deducted from said compensation, a reasonable sum, according to the proportion said work omitted may bear to the work herein first agreed to be done. And said district, or their proper agents, shall have a right to direct any additions or omissions as aforesaid, and the party of the other part shall be bound to comply with and perform the said directions.

[*Clause to refer to arbitration.*]

And lastly, it is hereby agreed between the parties aforesaid, that if any dispute shall happen between the said district or its agents, and the said A B, his heirs, executors, administrators or assigns, in relation to the buildings herein agreed to be erected, work to be done, the payment of the money, or concerning the value and expense of any work directed to be added or omitted as hereinbefore mentioned, or concerning any other matter or thing whatever, relating to the construction of this agreement, or the amount of any damages claimed by either party, under its provisions, or for any alleged violation thereof, then in such case such dispute shall, upon the demand of either party, be left to the award and determination of three indifferent persons, one to be appointed in writing by each of said parties, immediately thereafter, and a third to be appointed in writing by the two persons so first named. And the said parties hereby covenant and agree with each other, that they will severally abide by, perform and keep the award and determination of the said three persons, or any two of them, touching said disputes, provided said award be made under the hands and seals of said arbitrators, or any two of them, within   from the time of said reference.

In testimony whereof, the said A B hath hereto set his hand and seal, and said district have hereto affixed their seal, by the hands of   duly authorized for that purpose, who hath [or have] hereto also set their own hands.

Sealed and delivered in presence of   [L. S.]
      A B.

Names of committee or agents.   [L. S.]

Note.—If the district wishes a surety for the performance of a contract of A B, it may be taken by a bond, conditioned for the performance by A B, of the covenants and agreements in an instrument dated   [and then briefly describe it.]

---

15. *Vote of District to Tax.*

At the annual meeting of the legal voters of School District No. of the town of   held at   on   according to legal notice issued and signed by   and posted up at   for the five days previous required by law, [or, at a special meeting of, &c., called by, &c.]

Whereas, this district has voted to build a school-house in and for said district, [or to repair the district school-house,]

Voted, that for the purpose of defraying the expense thereof, a tax of the sum of   dollars be assessed upon, levied and collected from the ratable property in this district, in manner provided by law, the school committee of the town having approved of the amount of tax before mentioned for the purpose aforesaid, and that the assessment be made according to the estimate, apportionment and value affixed to said ratable property in the last assessment and tax bill made out by the town assessors, [or, according to the estimate, apportionment and value which shall be affixed to said ratable estates in the assessment and tax bill of this town which shall next be completed after the date of this vote.]

Note.— In case of laying a tax, it is important that the notice of the meeting should be legally given, and that evidence of the notice should be preserved.

All taxes must be voted and collected according to the present school act, all the former town and local acts being repealed, and it is best that every tax should be voted by *specific* sum and not by so much per cent.

On laying a tax, or on any question relating to the expenditure of money, those only are entitled to vote who shall have paid or are liable to pay taxes.

If the district vote to have their tax assessed according to the *last* town valuation, the trustee or trustees will immediately proceed to make out the tax bill accordingly. If there are any complaints of wrong valuation, it would be well for the district to postpone the tax until the *next* town assessment is completed, to give the parties an opportunity to be heard before the town assessors.

If any property within the district is assessed to any person, together with property out of the district, so that there is no separate valuation of that portion which may lie within the district lines, and in the other cases referred to in chap. 64, sec. 2, the trustees should apply in writing to one or more of the town assessors, living out of the district, stating the names of the parties so situated; and the assessor will immediately issue a notice, and at the expiration of the ten days, proceed to decide and apportion the valuation. The assessor should certify the facts upon the tax bill when made out. As the assessor is called upon to act in these cases solely upon business of the district, his fees should be paid by the district. The trustees should see that the assessor has taken his engagement before he acts in the case.

Persons must be taxed for personal property according to their residence when the assessment is made. The general rule as to taxation is, that personal property shall be taxed to the owner where he resides, and real estate where it lies. A few exceptions from this rule, made by statute, are hereafter referred to.

If any property has changed owners since the last town valuation, it of course must be assessed to the actual owners at the time the school-tax bill is made out. This is the reasonable construction of the law.

The following is an abstract of the existing tax laws of the State; but a collector, before proceeding to act, should always inquire if they have been altered or amended:

In assessing a tax, real and personal estate must be valued separately, and put in separate columns, and the assessors must distinguish those who give in a list. They may assess it either to the owner or occupant. It should not be assessed against a person deceased. If the last town assessment is defective in any legal requisites, the district may vote to go by the next assessment, and in the mean time endeavor to have them remedied.

Meeting-houses, school-houses, academies and colleges, the land on which they stand, and burial-grounds, are exempted from taxation. Buildings on leased land are to be deemed real estate. The custom-houses in Newport and Providence are exempt. No poll-tax can be laid for any purpose. It has been decided in Massachusetts, that a person residing on land ceded to the United States, and where the State has only reserved a right of serving process, is not taxable. (8 Mass. Rep. 72; 1 Metcalf, Rep. 680.) Machinery in cotton and woolen factories is to be taxed in the towns where located, in the same manner as if the owner resided there.

Personal property in trust, the income of which is to be paid by some other person, must be assessed to the trustee in the town where such other person resides, if in the State, but if such person lives out of the State, then it is to be taxed where the trustee, executor, &c., resides.

Personal property in the hands of executors, guardians, &c., is to be taxed to them in the town where the deceased dwelt or the ward resides.

Collection of Taxes.—The mode of distraining and selling personal property is pointed out in the revised statutes. The mode of notifying and selling land for taxes is also prescribed by law. If he find no real or personal estate, he may commit the body. If a person is taxed for more than one parcel of land, the whole tax may be collected out of any one parcel. If real estate is assessed to the tenant, the tenant's own real and personal estate is liable to be taken for the tax, and if that cannot be found, the land in his occupation is liable. A tax warrant remains in force until the whole tax is collected. The collector's fees are to be paid out of the district treasury, and will be five per cent., unless he makes a different agreement with the district. If the collector dies or resigns, the new collector will have power to complete the collection. The oath of the collector is admitted to prove a demand. Any district may offer a deduction to those who pay in time, or impose a percentage on those who do not.

Any person committed to jail for a tax, rate or assessment, may swear out in the same manner as if he was committed for town taxes. And any person assessed for tuition may take the poor debtor's oath before being committed.

The uniform, arms, ammunition and equipments of an officer or private in the militia, cannot be distrained for taxes. And household furniture, family stores, tools, &c., are in some cases protected from distress.

Owners of real estate or buildings sold for taxes, may redeem within six months after sale, on paying to the purchaser the amount paid therefor, with twenty per cent. in addition.

By the new school act, the trustees are to assess the taxes (except in the cases where an assessor is to be called on) and the trustees issue the warrants immediately to the collector. And the district may vote to have it collected by the town collector. Any person neglecting to appear before the assessor after notice given, has no remedy. Any tax or assessment not appealed from cannot be questioned in court afterwards. Provision is made for correcting errors

6

and reässessing a tax. As to cases of persons affected by a change of boundaries of a district, see tax in the index.

---

16. *Form of a Tax Bill.*

Assessment of the taxes upon the ratable estates in School District No.   of the town, &c., made by the trustees thereof, according to law, this   day of   A. D. 18   for the purpose of raising the sum of   dollars, according to a vote of said district, passed on the   day of   A. D. 18

Names.	Real.	Personal.	Total.	Tax.

NOTE.—The trustees should sign the tax bill. If the town assessors are applied to, it would be well to have them make their certificate at the foot of the tax bill, and sign it.

---

17. *District Treasurer's Bond.*

Know all men, that we, A B, of   county of   and State of Rhode Island and Providence Plantations, as principal, and C D, of   county of   and State aforesaid, as surety, [surety or sureties to the satisfaction of the district,] are firmly held and bound unto the School District No.   of the town of   and State aforesaid, in the full sum of [to be fixed by the district] to be paid to the said school district, or their assigns, to which we hereby jointly and severally bind ourselves, our several and respective heirs, executors and administrators.

Sealed and dated the   day of   A. D. 18

The condition of the foregoing obligation is, that whereas the said A B was, at a meeting of said school district, holden   appointed treasurer of said district. Now, if he shall faithfully discharge the duties of said office during his continuance therein, and at the expiration of his office he or his executors or administrators shall exhibit a true account, if required, and deliver over to his successor, or the order of the district, all books, papers and moneys belonging to the district, in his hands, then the above obligation is to be void, otherwise to remain in force.

Executed in presence of   [L. S.]

                                                          [L. S.]

Note.—It may be advisable for the treasurer to receive a formal certificate of appointment, or warrant, and then his engagement can be indorsed upon it. The above bond need not be given unless the district require it.

18. *District Collector's Bond.*

Know all men, that we, A B, of   State of Rhode Island and Providence Plantations, as principal, and C D, of   as surety, are firmly held and bound unto E F, of   treasurer of School District No.   in the town of   and State aforesaid, in the full sum of [to be fixed by the district, not exceeding double the tax] to be paid to said . his successors in said office, or assigns, to which we jointly bind ourselves, our several and respective heirs, executors and administrators.

Sealed and dated this   day of   A. D. 18

The condition of this obligation is, that whereas the said A B was, at a meeting of the legal voters of School District No.   of the town of   appointed collector of the rates and taxes assessed and to be assessed in, by, and upon said district, and the said A B has accepted said office ;. and whereas said district on the   day of, A. D. 18   voted that a tax of   be assessed on all the ratable property in said district, for the purpose of   and said tax has been legally assessed, and the trustee of said district hath issued his warrant to said collector, with said rate bill annexed, for the collection of said tax, the receipt of which said rate bill and warrant is hereby acknowledged, and by which said warrant, said tax is to be collected and paid over, on or before the   day of   A. D. 18 Now if the said A B shall faithfully perform and discharge said office and trust, and with diligence and fidelity, levy and collect, as far as may be done, all the taxes that have been, or may be so committed to him for collection, during his continuance in office, and he, his heirs, executors or administrators shall at all times on proper demand, render an account and pay over all the proceeds of such collections to the treasurer of said district, or his successors in office, according to the directions contained in the warrants for their collection, then this obligation is to be void, otherwise to remain in force.

Executed in presence of   [L. S.]
     [L. S.]

Note.—The collector need not give bond, unless required.

19.   *Warrant to collect a Tax.*

To A B, collector of taxes of School District No.   of the town
of   county of   and State of Rhode Island and Providence
Plantations :—GREETING.

You, having been appointed collector of taxes for said district, are
hereby, in the name of said State, authorized and required to proceed
and collect the tax specified in the annexed rate bill, according to law,
and to pay the same to the treasurer of the district, or to his successor in office ; and for so doing this shall be your sufficient warrant.

Given under my hand and seal, at   this   day of   A. D. 18

C. D.   [L. S.]

Trustee of said School District.

NOTE. The collector should also receive from the district clerk a warrant or formal certificate of election, which may be in substance according to the form No. 18.
And then his engagement can be certified upon the back.

The district should approve the sum and sureties of the bond, and the clerk should
certify the fact thereon.

20.   *Form of Tax Collector's Deed.*

To all to whom these presents may come. I, A B, of   county
of   and State of Rhode Island and Providence Plantations, collector of taxes of School District No.   in said town, send Greeting :—

Whereas the said school district, at a meeting duly notified, and
held on the   day of   A. D. 18   voted that a tax of   dollars
be assessed on the ratable property in said district, for the purpose
of   and said tax was afterwards, viz. : on the   day of
A. D. 18   assessed according to law, and the tax bill in due form
delivered to me the said collector, with a warrant attached thereto,
signed by the trustees, of said district, requiring me to proceed according to law and collect the said tax, and pay over the same to the
treasurer of the district, or to his successor in office, and whereas
C D, of   neglected to pay the tax assessed against him, and
expressed in the said tax bill, amounting to the sum of   dollars,
and in consequence thereof, I did on the   day of   levy said
warrant upon a certain lot or tract of land belonging to said C D, in
said district, and did advertise the same for sale according to law, at
two [or more] public places in said town, for twenty days previous
to sale, [and also in the   a newspaper printed in   ] and on

the   day of   A. D. 18   at   o'clock in the   noon, on the premises, being the time and place appointed, I proceeded to sell at auction so much of said land as was necessary to satisfy said tax and the incidental expenses, and E F, of   was the highest bidder therefor.

Now, know ye, that in consideration of the sum of   dollars, being the amount of said tax and expenses paid me by the said E F, I the said collector, do hereby give, grant, bargain, sell and convey unto the said E F, his heirs and assigns, all the right, title and interest which said C D, had at the time of assessing said tax, in and to the following described tract of land, situated in the district and town aforesaid, containing   acres, [more or less,] and bounded [describe] or however otherwise bounded, with all [buildings] and appurtenances, being so much of said land of the said C D, levied on as was necessary to satisfy said tax and expenses. To have and to hold the same to said E F, his heirs and assigns forever, subject to the right of redemption provided by law. And I, the said A B, for myself, my heirs, executors and administrators, do covenant with said E F, his heirs and assigns, that I [have given bond and] have advertised said property as hereinbefore stated, and have complied with the terms of the law regulating the collecting of taxes, in respect to said sale, as hereinbefore stated.

Witness my hand and seal, this   day of   A. D. 18
Signed, sealed and delivered in presence of

       A. B.   [L. S.]

Town of, &c.   A. D. 18   Before me the subscriber, appeared A B, collector of taxes of School District No.   of the town of   and acknowledged the foregoing to be his free act and deed, and his hand and seal to be thereunto affixed.

                               O. P.,
     Justice of the Peace, Notary Public or Town Clerk.

NOTE.—In case of unimproved lands owned by persons out of the State, and also of improved lands where neither the owner nor occupant lives in the State, notice of the sale must be given twenty days in a newspaper. The purchaser under a tax collector's deed should see that the law has been complied with, and that his evidence of advertising is preserved.

----

21.   *Form of a Rate-bill for Tuition, &c.*

Rate-bill or assessment of rates for tuition against the parents, guardians and employers, sending children to the district school, or

persons attending school, in School District No.   of the town
of   for the term of school commencing   and ending
made out this   day of   A. D. 18   towards the expenses of
tuition, fuel and other expenses.

Names of persons.	No. sent.	Time sent.	Assessment.

Signed

A. B. ⎫
C. D. ⎬ *Trustees.*
E. F. ⎭

NOTE.—This rate bill is to be collected in the same manner as the tax bill, and the same form will answer with a little variation to suit the case. Any poor person liable for tuition may, if the district or trustees refuse to exempt him, take the poor debtor's oath, either before or after being committed to jail.

---

22. *Form of a Lease.*

These articles of agreement made this   day of   A. D. 18
witness that A. B. of   doth hereby demise and let unto the School
District No.   of said town, (describe the room or building) with
the appurtenances, in consideration of the rents and covenants by
said school district herein mentioned to be performed, to have and
hold the same to the said school district and their assigns for the space
of   year, commencing on the   day of   A. D. 18   and
ending on the   day of   A. D. 18   for the purpose of keeping a district school therein, and holding such schools or lectures or
other literary meetings, or meetings of business, as the school committee or the officers of said district may deem advisable for promoting the cause of education. And the said district agrees to pay
therefor the sum of   per annum as rent, and at that rate for any
less time than a year, the payment to be made to the said A B, his
heirs or assigns, at his residence, on the last day of the year, [or on
the last day of each year in the term,] without any notice or demand
therefor, [provisions about repairs, loss by fire, &c., may be here inserted.] Witness the hand and seal of said A B, and the seal of the
said district hereto affixed by   · by said district duly authorized,
the day and year first above mentioned.

Sealed and executed in presence of

[L. S.]

[L. S.]

23. *Power of Attorney to take a Lease.*

Note.—The district may authorize a person to execute this lease for them by a vote as follows : " Voted, that the trustees of the district [or treasurer] be and they are hereby fully empowered to hire a building for the purpose of a school-house for the district [here specify the building, and fix the time and conditions or leave them at discretion,] and to make and execute the necessary contracts therefor, and to seal, deliver and acknowledge the same in the name and behalf of the district." If the lease is for a year or less time, it may save trouble to take the lease in the name of the trustees themselves. If the above is to be acknowledged, see the form of acknowledgment to No. 26.

---

24. *Deed to a School District.*

Know all men that I, A B, of   in the State of Rhode Island and Providence Plantations, in consideration of the sum of   paid me by C D, treasurer of School District No.   in the town of   and State aforesaid, the receipt of which I acknowledge and am therewith fully satisfied and paid, [if a gift, say, in consideration of my desire to aid and assist in diffusing the benefits of a good common school education among the inhabitants of School District No. &c., as the grantor pleases] do hereby give, grant, enfeoff, convey and confirm unto said school district and their assigns, a certain lot of land situated in said town of   [describe] or however otherwise bounded, with all the appurtenances and privileges thereto belonging, to have and to hold the same forever to said school district [and their assigns, but if there is a desire to prevent the lot ever being used for any other purpose, omit assigns and say, for the purpose of maintaining thereon a district school-house and its appurtenances, for the benefit of the district school of said district, and for no other use or purpose whatever.] And I, the said A B, do hereby for myself, my heirs, executors and administrators, covenant and engage to and with said school district [and their assigns] that the premises are free of all incumbrances, that I have good right to sell and convey as aforesaid, and that I, my heirs, executors and administrators shall and will forever warrant, secure and defend the premises to said school district [and their assigns or to and for the purpose aforesaid,] against the lawful claims of all persons whatsoever. And I, E F, wife of the said A B, for the consideration paid my said husband, hereby release unto said school district [and their assigns] all my right of dower in the premises. [If the premises are under mortgage, a release may be here inserted.] And I, G H, of   in consideration of the sum of   paid to me by   to my full satisfaction, do hereby give, grant, bargain, sell, assign and convey unto said school district, [and their assigns,] all the right, title and interest which I have in the premises by virtue of any mortgage deed thereof, [or of any other claim or title whatsoever.] In witness whereof we have hereunto set our hands and seals this   day of   A. D. 18

Signed, sealed and delivered in presence of   [L. S.]

[L. S.]

[L. S.]

State of   county of   town of   A. D. 18   This day personally appeared before me   and acknowledged the foregoing instrument to be   voluntary act and deed and   hand and seal to be thereunto affixed.

Before me, O P, Justice of the Peace, Notary Public or Town Clerk, (if executed in Rhode Island.)

NOTE.- If the land belong to a married woman, her name should be inserted as one of the grantors, and the deed altered accordingly. She must acknowledge separately from her husband. Use the words of the law in the certificate of acknowledgment. See Revised Statutes.

---

25. *Vote appointing an Attorney to sell Land belonging to the District.*

At a meeting of the legal voters of School District No.   of the town of   &c., notified as the law requires, and held at   on the   day of   A. D. 18

Voted, That A B, Treasurer of said School District, be and he is hereby appointed the agent and attorney of the district, to sell at his discretion, a certain lot of land, situated in and belonging to the district, containing   bounded   with the buildings and appurtenances, and with full power to affix the seal of the district to a deed or deeds conveying the same [with covenants of warranty or not, as the district may vote,] and in the name of the district to acknowledge and deliver the same, and receive the purchase-money, and give a full discharge therefor.

A true copy of record: Witness,

E. F., Clerk of said District.

26. *District Land Deed.*

Know all men, that the School District No.   of the town of
county of   State of Rhode Island and Providence Plantations, in
consideration of the sum of   paid to A B, treasurer of said district,
to and for the use of said district, by M N, of   the receipt of
which is hereby acknowledged, does hereby give, grant, bargain, sell
and convey unto the said M N, his heirs and assigns, all the right,
title and interest of said school district, in and to a lot of land situated
in said district, containing   bounded   or however otherwise
bounded, with all buildings and appurtenances, being the same lot
conveyed to said district by deed of H I. To have and to hold the
same to said M N, his heirs and assigns, forever. In testimony
whereof, the said school district have hereunto fixed their seal, by
the hands of said A B, their treasurer, duly appointed for that purpose, at a legal meeting of said district, and the said treasurer hath
hereunto affixed his own hand, this   day of   A. D. 18

A B, Treasurer as aforesaid.   [L. S.]
Signed and sealed in presence of

Acknowledgment.

State of Rhode Island and Providence Plantations, county of
town of   A. D. 18   The School District No.   of said town,
by A B, their treasurer and attorney for that purpose, by vote of
said district appointed, acknowledged the foregoing to be their voluntary act and deed, and their seal to be thereto affixed ; and the said
A B, treasurer and attorney as aforesaid, also acknowledged his own
hand affixed thereto, and that the same was the voluntary act and
deed of himself and of the said district.

Before me,   P Q,
Justice of the Peace, or Notary Public, or Town Clerk.

Note.—It will seldom, if ever, be advisable for a district to give any thing more
than a quitclaim deed. If they wish to insert any warranty, it would be best to
consult a well-informed attorney.

---

27. *Order for Money.*

To A B, town treasurer of the town of
Pay to C D, or order, the sum of   it being for keeping a district school in School District No.   in this town.

By order of the School Committee of the town.

Date.   E F, Chairman or Clerk.

7

---

28. *Notice of Appeal.*

To the school committee of the town of   [trustees of School District No.   in the town of   ]

I hereby notify you, that in conformity with the provisions of the laws regulating public schools, I appeal to A B, commissioner of public schools, from [here specify the vote or decision of the committee, trustees, or district, which is complained of.]

Signed,

Date.   C D.

A copy of this notice should be immediately served upon the clerk of the committee, clerk of the district, or upon the trustee, trustees or inspector, who have done the act complained of. And a notice of the appeal should be immediately forwarded to the commissioner, which may be as follows :

An Appeal.

To A B, commissioner of public schools of the State of Rhode Island and Providence Plantations :

Whereas, the school committee, [trustees, of School District No. of the town of   No.   ] did at a meeting on the   day of A. D. 18   pass a vote—[here copy or insert the substance, as nearly as can be procured.] I, the subscriber, according to law, do hereby appeal to you from said vote or decision, and claim that the same may be reversed. [Here state plainly and briefly the reasons.]

Signed,

---

29. *Vote of District to establish a Secondary School.*

Voted, That this district will unite with School District No.   of this town, [or in the adjoining town of   ] in the establishment of a secondary school, according to the provisions of laws regulating public schools, passed January session, A. D. 1857, for the common benefit of both said districts ; provided said School District No. shall also give their consent thereto, [within   from this date], and that the clerk of the district furnish a certified copy of this vote to said

School District No.   and also to the school committee that, [if said district consents] they may take the necessary measures for establishing said school.

---

30.   *Vote of School Committee to form Joint District.*

Voted, [the school committee of the town of   concurring herewith] that a joint district be formed according to the provisions of the acts relating to public schools, to consist of School District No. of this town, and School District No.   of said town of   and that said districts shall constitute a joint district from the time that the school committee of said town of   shall concur herewith [or if they have already passed a similar vote say, from and after the passage of this vote.]

Voted further, that the chairman be authorized, in conjunction with the school committee of said town of   to cause notices to be posted up· [in one or more places in each of the two districts—specify them] for the first meeting of said joint district, to be held at on   at   o'clock in the   noon [or to be held at such time and place as he may agree upon with the school committee of said town of   ] and that the clerk of the committee furnish a certified copy of this vote to the school committee of the said town of

Note.—A notice signed by the chairman of each committee should be posted up in one or more places in each district. After trustees are elected, they will notify the subsequent meetings.

---

31.   *Vote prescribing Form of District Seal.*

Voted, That the clerk of the district cause to be made a seal for the use of the district, with the figure of   engraven thereon, and the letters or inscription   around its margin, and that the same is hereby adopted, and declared to be the common seal of this corporation, and shall be kept by the clerk of the district.

Note.—Every town, district, or other corporation, shall have a common seal, with a suitable device; but if they have no regular seal, any seal may be affixed to any instrument by their authority, for instance a piece of paper attached by a wafer will be considered to be their seal.

32. *Returns from School Committee to the Commissioner of Public Schools.*

STATEMENT of Expenditures of the Public Schools of for the year ending May 1, 18

Funds remaining unexpended of last year's money, . $
Received from State treasury, ...
    "   " town tax, ...
    "   " registry and militia taxes, . .
    "   " rate bills, . . .
    "   " income of funds, . . .
    "   " other sources, . . .

                   Total resources, . . . $

Expended for support of schools (except building and repairing school-houses,) . . . . $
Expended for building and repairing of school-houses, .
Amount voted by the town for next year, . . .

      Statistics of each separate School in

Each district or separate school in the town should be reported for both the winter and summer schools—indeed for every term—as follows:

    Amount of money expended on the school-house,
    Whole No. of boys attending,
       "   " girls "
    Total No. of scholars "
    Average No. of scholars attending,
    Male or female teacher,
    Wages per month, including board,
    Teacher's name,
    Length of school in weeks,
    No. of scholars attending under 4,
       "   "   " over 15,
    Amount of money from State's appropriation,
       "   "   " town's "
       "   "   " rate bills,
       "   "   " taxes,

    We, the school committee of the town of   in conformity with the laws relating to public schools, do certify that the foregoing form and blank for town returns prescribed by the commissioner of public schools have been filled with due diligence and accuracy, and that the above is a true statement of the moneys received from all sources and applied to the support of public schools for the year ending May 1, 18

---

33. *Form of District Return prescribed by the Commissioner of Public Schools, October, 1855.*

The following is the form prescribed by the first commissioner, Mr. Barnard, and is the one now used. The present commissioner has been several times urged to prepare a shorter form. But on the best consideration he has been able to give the subject, he is satisfied that it is most for the good of the schools to retain the existing form. A trustee, having all this information himself, may consider it trifling ; but it is all of importance to the school committee. Especially should exact returns of the attendance, studies and books be insisted on. By these the committee can ascertain whether improper books are used, and whether the teacher exercises proper judgment as to the studies and classification of his scholars. The trustee need have no trouble with it, if he will only require the teacher to fill it out, and there is nothing in the return but what the teacher can easily answer. I have seen instances of returns filled out by teachers in a manner and temper highly discreditable to them. No return should be allowed by a trustee or committee, unless the questions are answered in a respectful manner.

NOTE.—When there are separate schools kept at different times in the year, a separate return is to be made for each school, but the items included in the divisions I. II. III. VII. and IX. need be returned but once a year, and the items printed in italics need not be returned, except when specially required.

RETURN respecting the Public Schools in District No.   in town of   for term   commencing   18   and ending   18

I. NAME, SIZE, POPULATION, AND PROPERTY VALUATION OF THE DISTRICT.

Local or neighborhood name,
Territorial extent or size of district, length,   breadth,
Number of families residing in district,
     "   "   *engaged in agriculture,*
     "   "   "   *trade or shop-keeping,*
     "   "   "   *mechanics' shops,*

Number of families engaged in factories or mills,
    "   "   "   *navigation,*
    " *clergymen,*   *lawyers,*   *physicians,*
Number of inhabitants of all ages,   *Do. under 21 years,*
                              Do. between 5 and 15,
                              Do. under 5,
Whole number of voters,   *Do. tax-paying voters,*
Amount of valuation of taxable property in the district,

II. Pecuniary Resources.

Amount of State and town money actually expended during the present year. $

Amount of money raised by tax during the present year, on property of district, to purchase or build school-house, site, &c., $

Amount of money raised by tax during the present year, on property of district, to repair or furnish old house, $

Amount of money raised by tax during the present year, on property of district, to purchase maps, globes, and other apparatus, $

Amount of money raised by tax during the present year, on property of district, for teachers' wages, $ for board, $ for fuel, $

Aggregate amount of money raised *by tax on other property* of the district, during the year, for all purposes, $

Aggregate amount raised by rate, or tuition bill, for teachers' wages and board, fuel and other purposes, during the year, $

Amount given by individuals for any purpose during the year, $

Amount received from income of any land or fund, during the year, $

Aggregate amount of money expended for all purposes for the school year ending May, 18

III. School-Houses.

Place where the school is kept—in school-house,
       in building built or used for other purposes,
Date when the school-house was built,   *first cost,* $
When last thoroughly repaired,   *and at what expense,* $
By whom now owned, by district,   *town,*   *proprietors,*
Furnished with a suitable play-ground,   *and out-building,*
Material and condition of the building—material,   *condition,*
    [good, ordinary, bad,]
Provided with scraper,   *mat,*   *water-pail and cup,*   *sink,*
    basin, and towel,   *old broom for feet,*

Provided with pegs, hooks or shelves,   broom and dust-brush,
Number of school rooms and size of each,   length,   width,
height,
Arrangement for desks,
   " *seats,*
   " *ventilation,*
   " *warming,*
Provided with wood-shed or shelter for fuel,   shovel and tongs, &c.,
      thermometer,
Provided with bell,   with globe,   with clock,   hand-bell for
teacher,   Do. with blackboard, the size, [if any,]
Provided with map of Rhode Island,   Do. with outline maps,
Do. with geometrical solids,

IV. ATTENDANCE, LENGTH OF SCHOOL TERM.

Number of families who sent children to the school—belonging to
 district,
Number of families who sent children to the school—from out of the
 district,
Number of scholars of all ages registered during term—belonging to
 district, boys, girls,
Number of scholars of all ages registered during term—from out of
 the district, boys, girls,
Number of scholars over 15 years of age, boys, girls,
 " " under 5 years, boys, girls,
Length of school term in half days, Do. in weeks [10 half days.]
 Do. in months, [4 weeks,]
Number of scholars who attend three-fourths of the term and
 more,
Number of scholars who attend one-half of the term and more,
 " " " less than one-half " "
 " " " less than one-fourth " "
Average daily attendance of the school during the term,
Number of scholars belonging to the district at school in other dis-
 tricts or towns,

V. STUDIES AND CLASSES.

No. of scholars who commenced this term in Alphabet,
No. of scholars who attended during the whole term to Primer or
 Spelling Book, exclusively,
No. of scholars in Spelling, (not including scholars in Spelling Book,)
 No. of classes in,

No. of scholars in Reading, (not including scholars in Spelling Book,)
 No. of classes in,
No. of scholars in Geography, No. of classes in,
No. who draw maps,
No. of scholars in Grammar, No. of classes in,
No of scholars in History of the United States, No. of classes
 in,
No. of scholars in general History, No. of classes in,
No. of scholars in Etymology, or Analysis of Language, No. of
 classes in,
No. of scholars in Definitions, No. of classes in,
 " " Mental Arithmetic, No. of classes in,
 " " Written Arithmetic, No. of classes in,
 " " attending to Penmanship, No. of classes in,
 " " in Book-Keeping. No. of classes in,
 " " in Algebra, No. of classes in,
 " " in Geometry, No. of classes in,
 " " in Natural Philosophy, Classes in,
 " " in Physiology, Classes in,
 " " attending to drawing, Do. Composition,
Do. in Declamation, Do. who engage in Vocal Music,
No. of scholars in other studies, specifying the same,
 " " not provided with all books necessary in the studies
 pursued by them, not provided with slate,

VI. Books.

Name of each kind of Text-Book used in the school, and the number
 of copies of each kind,
Dictionary,
Primer,
Spelling Book,
Reading,
Penmanship and Book-Keeping,
Mental Arithmetic,
Written Arithmetic,
Geography,
Grammar,
History,
Other studies,

VII. Teachers.

Name and age of teacher,
Place (town and State) of birth,

Place (town and State) of residence,
Date of certificate, and by whom signed,
Number of terms, or years, of experience as a teacher in any school,
Number of terms, or years, of experience as a teacher in this school
  before the present term,
Compensation per month in money,
Aggregate amount in money for term,
Is the teacher boarded by the district in addition to his money wages?
  Or does he board himself out of his wages?
Arrangement for board—board round,   At one place,
If boarded by district, the amount paid in money for board,

VIII. Supervision or Visitation.

Number of visits from trustees,   From town committee,
From county inspector,   From parents and others,

IX. Private Schools, Lyceums, &c.

Number and grade of private or select school, kept in the district
  during the term,
Number of pupils attending,   Rate of tuition per term,
Name of any lyceum, debating society, or library, with date of establishment, number of members, books, &c.,

X. Names of Officers of the District.

Trustees,
Clerk,
Treasurer,
Collector,

To the School Committee of the Town of

We, the trustees of School District No.   in said town, in conformity with the laws relating to public schools, do certify that the
foregoing form of district return, prescribed by the commissioner of
public schools, has been filled up with due diligence and accuracy;
and that the money designated "teachers' money," received from
the treasurer of the town for the year previous to the first day of
May, 18   was applied to the wages of teachers, and for no other
purpose whatever.

Dated at   18

} *Trustees.*

8

34.   *Specimens of Rules and Regulations to be adopted by School
      Committees for the government of Public Schools.*

We give below, 1st, the rules adopted by the school committee of
Smithfield, A. D. 1846 ; 2d, the rules adopted in North and South
Kingstown, and some other towns ; 3d, extracts from the school regu-
lations of the town of Portsmouth.

I.

*Regulations for the government of the Public Schools in the town of
Smithfield.*

PREAMBLE.

Teachers and candidates for teachers in the public schools, previous
to entering upon their engagements, should consider it of great importance to become familiar with some of the most approved plans of
teaching and governing a school ; and should endeavor, as far as possible, to possess themselves of definite ideas in regard to the solemn
duties and responsibilities of their profession.

And in order to aid and assist them in establishing a uniform and
systematic course of instruction and discipline, the committee would
respectfully submit the following

RULES.

1.   All the teachers of the public schools are required to be at their
respective school-rooms and to ring the bell from ten to fifteen minutes before the time of commencing the school in the morning and in
the afternoon, and they shall require the pupils, as they enter the
room, to be seated in an orderly manner, and prepare for study.

2.   The bell shall again be struck, or the hand-bell rung, *precisely*
at the specified time for beginning the school, as a *signal* for commencing the exercises—previous to which all the scholars are expected
to be present and to have made all needful preparations for carrying
on the business of the school, in order to prevent all unnecessary
movement after the exercises commence.

3.   All the public schools shall be opened in the morning by reading a portion of the Scriptures, which may be done by the teacher
alone, or in connection with the older pupils—the whole school being
required at the same time to suspend all other subjects and to give
proper and respectful attention ; and this exercise may be followed
by prayer or not, at the discretion of the teacher.

4. Every scholar who comes in after the second bell rings, must present a satisfactory excuse ; and all who cannot do so, shall be considered delinquent, and marked tardy on the teacher's register, subject to examination by parents, trustees and school committee.

5. No teacher shall permit whispering or talking in school, or allow the scholars to leave or change their seats, or to have communication with each other in school time, without permission, but shall strive to maintain that good order and thorough discipline which are absolutely essential to the welfare of the school.

6. It shall be the duty of teachers to guard the conduct of scholars, not only in the hours of school, but at recess, and on their way to and from school, and to extend at all times a watchful care over their morals and manners, endeavoring to inculcate those virtues which lay a sure foundation for future usefulness and happiness.

7. The government and discipline of the school should be of a mild and parental character. The teacher should use his best exertions to bring scholars to obedience and a sense of duty, by mild measures and kind influences ; and in cases where corporal punishment seems absolutely necessary, it should be inflicted with judgment and discretion, and in general not in presence of the school.

8. Teachers should ever avoid those low, degrading and improper forms of punishment, such as tying up scholars' hands and feet, compelling them to hold a weight in their hands with their arms extended, pinching, pulling and wringing their ears, cheeks and arms, and other similar modes, which are sometimes used, as the committee are decidedly of the opinion that a judicious teacher will find other methods of governing more consistent and more effectual.

9. In case of obstinate disobedience or wilful violation of order, a teacher may suspend a pupil from school for the time being, by informing the parents or guardians and school committee thereof, and readmit him on satisfactory evidence of amendment ; or such pupil may, at the discretion of the teacher, be referred directly to the committee, to be dealt with as their judgment and legal authority shall dictate.

10. The teachers shall classify the pupils of their respective schools according to their age and attainments, irrespective of rank or wealth, and shall assign them such lessons as seem best adapted to their capacities, and render them all possible aid and assistance, without distinction and without partiality.

11. For the purpose of preserving that system and order so essential to a well-regulated school, and securing to the pupils a thorough knowledge of the subjects pursued, there should be a specified time

for every exercise, and a certain portion of time devoted to it; and in no case should any one recitation interfere with the time appropriated to another; and whatever the exercise may be, it should receive, for the time, the immediate and, as far as practicable, the exclusive attention of the teacher.

12. No child under the age of four years shall be received as a scholar in a district school, unless there be an assistant teacher or a primary department.

13. Exercises in declamation and composition shall be practiced by the older and more advanced pupils, at the judgment of the teacher, under the advice of the committee.

14. Singing may be encouraged, and, as far as practicable, taught in all the schools, not only for its direct intellectual and moral uses, but as a healthy exercise of the lungs, an agreeable recreation to the pupils, and an auxiliary in good government.

15. Needle-work shall be allowed in the primary schools.

16. The teacher may employ the older scholars, under his direction, in the management of the school, when it can be done without disadvantage to them or to the good order of the schools.

17. No teacher shall use or encourage the use of any other books than those recommended by the committee, without their approbation.

18. There shall be a recess of at least fifteen minutes in the middle of every half day; but the primary schools may have a recess of ten minutes every hour; at the discretion of the teacher.

19. It shall be the duty of teachers to see that fires are made in cold weather, in their respective school-rooms, at a seasonable hour to render them warm and comfortable by school time; to take care that their rooms are properly swept and dusted; and that a due regard to neatness and order is observed, both in and around the school-house.

20. As pure air of a proper temperature is indispensable to health and comfort, teachers cannot be too careful in giving attention to these things. If the room has no ventilator, the doors and windows should be opened before and after school, to permit a free and healthful circulation of air; and the temperature should be regulated by a thermometer suspended five or six feet from the floor, in such a position as to indicate as near as possible the average temperature, and should be kept at about sixty-five degrees Fahrenheit.

21. The teachers shall take care that the school-houses, tables, desks, and apparatus in the same, and all the public property intrusted to their charge, be not cut, scratched, marked, or injured or defaced in any manner whatever. And it shall be the duty of the teachers to give prompt notice to one or more of the trustees, of any repairs that may be needed.

22. Every teacher shall keep a record of all the recitations of every class; and of the manner in which every member of the class shall acquit himself in his recitation—using figures or otherwise to mark degrees of merit. Also, every act of disobedience or violation of order, shall be noted; and the registers shall be at all times subject to the inspection of parents, trustees and the school committee.

23. The following shall be the construction of teachers' engagements, unless otherwise specified in the written contract. They shall teach six hours every day, including the recess, and shall divide the day into two sessions, with at least one hour intermission. They shall teach every day in the week, except Saturday and Sunday, and four weeks for a month; and they may dismiss the school on the fourth of July, on Christmas, and on days of public fast and thanksgiving, and one day out of every month for the purpose of attending a teacher's institute, or for visiting schools.

PUPILS.

24. Good morals being of the first importance, and essential to their progress in useful knowledge, the pupils are strictly enjoined to avoid all vulgarity and profanity, falsehood and deceit, and every wicked and disgraceful practice; to conduct themselves in a sober, orderly and decent manner, both in and out of school; .to be diligent and attentive to their studies; to treat each other politely and kindly in all their intercourse; to respect and obey all orders of their teachers in relation to their conduct and studies, and to be punctual and constant in their daily attendance.

25. Every pupil who shall, *accidentally or otherwise*, injure any school property, whether fences, gates, trees or shrubs, or any building or any part thereof; or break any window glass, or injure or destroy any instrument, apparatus or furniture belonging to the school, shall be liable to pay all damages.

26. Every pupil who shall anywhere on or around the school premises, use or write any profane or unchaste language, or shall draw any obscene pictures or representations, or cut, mark, or otherwise *intentionally* deface any school furniture or buildings, or any property whatsoever belonging to the school estate, shall be punished in proportion to the nature and extent of the offence, and shall be liable to the action of the civil law.

27. No scholar of either sex shall be permitted to enter any part of the yard or buildings appropriated to the other, without the teacher's permission.

28. Smoking and chewing tobacco in the school-house or upon the school premises, are strictly prohibited.

29. The scholars shall pass through the streets on their way to and from the school in an orderly and becoming manner; shall clean the mud and dirt from their feet on entering the school-room; and take their seats in a quiet and respectful manner, as soon as convenient after the first bell rings; and shall take proper care that their books, desks, and the floor around them, are kept clean and in good order.

30. It is expected that all the scholars who enjoy the advantages of public schools, will give proper attention to the cleanliness of their persons, and the neatness and decency of their clothes—not only for the moral effect of the habit of neatness and order, but that the pupils may be at all times prepared, both in conduct and external appearance, to receive their friends and visitors in a respectable manner; and to render the school-room pleasant, comfortable and happy for teachers and scholars.

31. No scholar should try to hide the misconduct of his school-fellows, or screen them from justice; but it shall be the duty of every pupil who knows of any bad conduct, or violation of order, committed without the knowledge of the instructor, to the disgrace and injury of the school, to inform the teacher thereof, and to do all in his power to discourage and discountenance improper behavior in others, and to assist the teacher in restoring good order and sustaining the reputation of the school.

32. Every teacher shall keep a copy of these rules and regulations posted up in the school-room, and shall cause the same to be read aloud in school at least once in every month; and in case of any difficulty in carrying out these regulations, or in the government and discipline of the school, it shall be the duty of the teacher to apply immediately to the committee for advice and direction.

II.

Regulations for government of Public Schools, adopted in North and South Kingstown, &c.

TEACHERS.

1. Every person, before being employed to teach in any school supported wholly or in part by public money, shall be found qualified according to law; and for any immoral or grossly improper conduct, or, for refusing to comply with the regulations of the school committee, or the requests of the commissioner of public schools, shall be dismissed.

2. The teachers are expected to make the teaching of their school the main business, to give to it their best thoughts and energies, and to devote themselves to it to the exclusion of all other regular employment. And it is recommended that frequent meetings of the teachers be held for the purpose of personal improvement and of giving efficiency to the system of instruction, which meetings will be attended once a month by a committee of the board.

3. It shall be the duty of the teachers to fill all blanks, and make such returns as may be required of them by law and by the school committee or trustees; and to give notice to the school committee, of the time when the term will begin and close, so that the school may be visited according to law; and any teacher who shall for the space of weeks neglect to give notice as aforesaid, shall forfeit his pay for that time, unless he renders a satisfactory excuse.

4. In cases of difficulty in the discharge of their official duties, or when they may desire any temporary indulgence, the teachers shall apply to the trustees or committee for advice and direction.

5. The teachers are required to be at their respective school-houses, at least fifteen minutes before the specified time for beginning the school in the morning and in the afternoon; and to open their respective school-rooms, for the reception of pupils, subject to all the rules of order for school hours, as soon as they enter the rooms.

6. The teachers shall enroll the names of scholars as they enter the school—and cause all cases of absence and tardiness to be marked every morning and afternoon, and any withdrawal from school before the hour for closing, except in case of sickness, or upon a request stated in writing or in person, by the parent or guardian, shall be regarded as an absence.

7. As regularity and punctuality of attendance are indispensable to the success of a school, it is important to maintain the principle that necessity alone can justify absence. Sickness, domestic affliction, and absence from town are regarded as the only legitimate cause of absence. All other cases must be considered as in violation of rule, and deriving their only sanction from the private authority of a parent or guardian. In every instance of absence, a written excuse or personal explanation shall be required of the parent, master or guardian, on the return of the pupil to school.

8. The teachers in each school shall put the pupils into separate classes according to their age and attainments; and shall teach them such portions of the prescribed studies as in their judgment it shall be most suitable for each class to pursue; and each scholar shall be

confined to the studies of his class, unless for good reasons an exception be made by the teacher under the advice, or with the approbation of the committee.

9. It shall be the duty of the teachers to use their best endeavors to impress upon the minds of the youth committed to their care and instruction, the principles of piety, justice, and a sacred regard to truth, love to their country, humanity and universal benevolence, sobriety, industry, frugality, chastity, moderation, temperance, and those other virtues which are the ornament of human society, and the basis upon which a republican constitution is founded ; and they shall endeavor to lead their pupils, as their ages and capacities will allow, into a clear understanding of the tendency of these virtues to preserve and perfect a republican constitution, and secure the blessings of liberty, as well as to promote their own happiness ; and also to point out to them the evil tendency of the opposite vices. [*From Laws of Massachusetts.*]

10. It is expected that the teachers will exercise a general inspection over the conduct of the scholars, not only while in school, but also during their recess, while in the aisles and yards, and while coming to and returning from school.

11. It is recommended that the school be opened by reading a portion of the Bible, which may be read, either separately by the teachers, or by the scholars, or by both in connection ; but no scholar shall be required to engage in this exercise against the expressed wishes of the parent or guardian.

12. The teachers shall practise such discipline in the schools as would be exercised by a kind, judicious parent in his family, and shall avoid corporal punishment in all cases where order can be preserved by milder measures ; and they shall keep a faithful account of all punishments and the offences for which they are inflicted—subject to examination by the school committee, or trustees.

13. For violent opposition, or gross immorality or indecency, or contagious disease, a teacher may exclude a pupil from school for the time ; and in all such cases, shall forthwith give information in writing, of the cause thereof, to the parents or guardian, and to the school committee.

14. Whenever the example of any scholar shall be such as to be dangerous to the morality of the other scholars or the good order of the school, and there is no hope of reformation, the teacher shall report the case to the school committee for their advice and decision.

15. The teachers shall exert themselves, under the advice of the committee, to impart a knowledge of the English language, (including

orthography, etymology, pronunciation, definitions, composition, grammar and reading,) writing, mental and written arithmetic, geography, and the history of the United States.

16.   The following books are recommended to be used in the public schools: no teacher shall permit the scholars to use any keys to arithmetics or other mathematical works.

The following text-books shall be used in the studies specified:

[Here insert the names of such books as have been prescribed, or recommended, as the case may be, by the school committee.]

17.   In case any scholar is not provided with the proper books, the teacher shall inform the parent, guardian or master thereof; and if such parent, guardian or master shall not within one week provide proper books, the teacher shall inform the trustees of the district, who shall provide the same in manner prescribed by law.

18.   The teacher shall endeavor to combine the use of oral instruction and familiar explanations with the recitation from the prescribed books, especially on the subject of morals and manners.

19.   Needle work may be allowed in the primary schools.

20.   Exercises in declamation shall take place at suitable times at the discretion of the teacher under the advice of the committee.

21.   Singing shall be encouraged, and, as far as practicable, taught in all the schools, not only for its direct intellectual and moral uses, but as a healthy exercise of the lungs, an agreeable recreation to the pupils, and an auxiliary in school government; but no one shall be required to engage in it against the wishes of his parents.

22.   The teacher may, under the advice of the visiting committee, occasionally employ the older scholars to assist under his direction in the management of the school when they are capable, and when it can be done without disadvantage to them or to the good order of the school.

23.   Every teacher shall keep a record of all the recitations of every class, and of the manner in which every member of the class shall acquit himself in his recitations, using figures or otherwise to mark degrees of merit, and shall exhibit the same to the parents or guardians, committee or trustee, when required.

24.   It is recommended that there shall be a recess of at least ten minutes in every half day for the older scholars, and of ten minutes in every hour, for the younger.

25.   The teachers shall give vigilant attention to the ventilation and temperature of their rooms, causing those that have been occupied to be opened and aired each morning and afternoon, at the times

of recess, and at the end of school hours; and they shall use all proper means to avoid those injurious extremes of heat and cold, which negligence might induce.

26. The teachers shall take care that their rooms and entries are kept neat and clean, and swept as often as necessary, and that they be dusted every day.

27. The teachers shall take care that the school-houses, the apparatus in the same, and all the public property intrusted to their charge, be not defaced or otherwise injured by the scholars; and it shall be the duty of the teachers to give prompt notice, to one or more of the trustees, of any repairs or supplies that may be needed; and they may prescribe such rules for the use of the yards and out-buildings connected with the school-houses, as shall insure their being kept in a neat and proper condition, and shall examine them as often as may be necessary for such purpose; and they shall be held responsible for any want of neatness or cleanliness about their premises.

28. The following rules shall be observed by all teachers unless otherwise specified in their written contract :—they shall teach six hours every day, including the recess, and shall divide the day into two sessions with at least one hour intermission in the middle of the day;—they shall teach every day in the week, except Saturday and Sunday, and four weeks for a month. They may dismiss the school on the Fourth of July, on Christmas, and days of public fast and thanksgiving, and for the purpose of attending a Teachers' Institute, and such other meetings as the commissioner of public schools may appoint and invite the attendance of the teachers.

PUPILS.

29. Good morals being of the first importance, and essential to their progress in useful knowledge, the pupils are strictly enjoined to avoid idleness and profanity, falsehood and deceit, and every wicked and disgraceful practice, and to conduct themselves in a sober, orderly and decent manner, both in and out of school; to obey all orders of their teachers in relation to their conduct and studies, and to be punctual and constant in daily attendance.

30. The scholars must scrape their feet on the scraper, and wipe them on every mat they pass over on their way to the school-room; they must hang their hats, caps and overcoats on the hooks, or deposit them on the shelves appropriated to each respectively; and must be held responsible for the neatness of their own desks and the floor nearest to their seat, and for the good order of their books and stationery.

31. No scholar who comes to school without proper attention having been given to the cleanliness of his person and of his dress, or whose clothes are not properly repaired, shall be permitted to remain in school.

32. Every pupil who shall anywhere on or around the school premises, use or write any profane or unchaste language, or shall draw any obscene pictures or representations, or cut, mark, or otherwise *intentionally* deface any school furniture or buildings, inside or out, or any property whatsoever belonging to the school estate, shall be punished in proportion to the nature and extent of the offence, and shall be liable to the action of the civil law.

33. Every pupil who shall, *accidentally or otherwise*, injure any school property, whether fences, gates, trees or shrubs, or any building or any part thereof; or break any window glass, or injure or destroy any instrument, apparatus or furniture belonging to the school, shall be liable to pay in full for all damage he has done.

34. All the scholars shall leave school in good order and quietly, as soon as dismissed, unless permitted by the teacher to remain; and all unnecessary noise in or around the school-house is prohibited. The throwing of sticks, stones or other missiles in or near the school-house, and the knocking off of caps or hats are strictly prohibited.

35. No scholar of either sex shall be permitted to enter that part of the yard and buildings appropriated to the other, without the teacher's permission.

36. Smoking and chewing tobacco in the school-house or upon the school premises, are forbidden.

37. There shall be a return made from every school supported in whole or in part by the public money, to the school committee, according to the form published by the commissioner of public schools, and with such additional items of information as the commissioner or committee may from time to time require. And if there be summer and winter schools, or there be two or more schools of the same or a different grade, a separate account shall be given of each school.

38. Every teacher shall keep a copy of these rules and regulations posted up in the school-room, and shall cause the same to be read aloud in school at least once in every month.

A true copy: Witness,

III.

The following are extracts from the regulations of the school committee of Portsmouth, which were drawn up by Thomas R. Hazard, Esq.:

Sec. 1.   It shall be the teacher's duty to act as librarian, and to adopt regulations from time to time for the security and useful application of the books ; subject to the approval of any committee which may be appointed by the district for that purpose.

Sec. 2.   It shall be required of the teacher to read aloud to his pupils, either at the commencement or close of the school, in suitable sections, the constitution of the United States, and of the State of Rhode Island, and to encourage his pupils in the perusal of such works as may be furnished the school library and approved of by the district, as may treat on commerce, finance, agriculture, manufactures, the mechanic arts, history of the law of nations as applicable in their intercourse with each other, and on such other subjects as may tend to qualify them to exercise that important and responsible trust, upon the faithful and upright discharge of which the very existence of their country may yet depend—" the right of suffrage."

Sec. 3.   It shall be the teacher's duty not only to cultivate the intellects of his pupils, but he shall seek proper occasions to promote their moral progress and improvement by discouraging the expansion of evil propensities ; and instilling into their minds every virtuous and elevated sentiment : such as at all times to adhere rigidly to the truth, both in heart and word, without regard to consequences : that they maintain a strict regard to the rights and feelings of others ; and that they cultivate friendly and compassionate sentiments one towards another, and to all living creatures ; that they ever abstain from inflicting unnecessary pain or death on any part of the animal creation ; and finally, that they live in conformity with that comprehensive injunction of the Saviour of men, and which includes every duty of man to his fellow man, " to do unto others as we would that they should do unto us."

MISCELLANEOUS.

MORAL INSTRUCTION,

Should by all means be inculcated by the teacher, but yet so as to avoid all sectarian comments or bias.

The rule laid down in the laws of the State of Massachusetts, while it points out and inculcates the duty of the teacher to give moral instruction, is carefully drawn to avoid giving countenance to any attempt to impart sectarian instruction.

"It shall be the duty of the teachers to use their best endeavors to impress upon the minds of the youth committed to their care and instruction, the principles of piety, justice, and a sacred regard to truth, love to their country, humanity and universal benevolence, sobriety, industry, frugality, chastity, moderation, temperance, and those other virtues which are the ornament of human society and the basis upon which a republican constitution is founded; and they shall endeavor to lead their pupils, as their ages and capacities will allow, into a clear understanding of the tendencies of these virtues to preserve and perfect a republican constitution and secure the blessings of liberty, as well as to promote their own happiness; and also to point out to them the evil tendency of the opposite vices."

READING THE BIBLE AND PRAYING IN SCHOOLS.

The constitution and laws of the State give no power to a school committee, nor is there any authority in the State by which the reading of the Bible or praying in school, either at the opening or at the close, can be commanded and enforced. On the other hand, the spirit of the constitution, and the neglect of the law to specify any penalty for so opening or closing a school, or to appoint or allow any officer to take notice of such an act, do as clearly show that there can be no compulsory exclusion of such reading and praying from our public schools. The whole matter must be regulated by the consciences of the teachers and inhabitants of the districts, and by the general consent of the community. Statute law and school committees' regulations can enforce neither the use nor disuse of such devotional exercises. School committees may recommend, but they can go no further.

It is believed to be the general sentiment of the people of Rhode Island, that this matter shall be left to the conscience of the teacher ; and it is expected, that if he read the Bible as an opening exercise, he shall read such parts as are not controverted or disputed, but such as are purely or chiefly devotional ; and if he pray at the opening of his school, he shall be very brief, and conform as nearly to the model of the Lord's Prayer as the nature of the case will admit. And in all this, he is bound to respect the conscientious scruples of the parents of the children before him, as he would have his own conscientious scruples respected by them in turn ; always, of course, taking care that in the means he uses to show his respect for the consciences of others, he does not violate the law of his own conscience.

Below is the form of prayer allowed by law to be used in the public schools of Canada. It will be found comprehensive and appropriate, and undoubtedly will be very generally acceptable to the community. It is given as a sample, like the samples of school rules and regulations previously given in these pages, and not as a form by any means prescribed, or even recommended to be used to the exclusion of any other.

OPENING AND CLOSING EXERCISES OF EACH DAY.

1. With a view to secure the Divine blessing, and to impress upon the pupils the importance of religious duties, and their entire dependence on their Maker, the council of public instruction recommend that the daily exercises of each grammar-school be opened and closed by reading a portion of Scripture and by prayer. The Lord's Prayer, alone, or the forms of prayer hereto annexed, may be used, or any other prayer preferred by the board of trustees and headmaster of each grammar-school. But the Lord's Prayer shall form a part of the opening exercises ; and the ten commandments shall be taught to all the pupils, and shall be repeated at least once a week. But no pupil shall be compelled to be present at these exercises against the wish of his parent or guardian, expressed in writing to the head-master of the school.

FORMS OF PRAYER.

I. BEFORE ENTERING UPON THE BUSINESS OF THE DAY.

O Lord our Heavenly Father, Almighty and Everlasting God, who hath safely brought us to the beginning of this day, defend us in the same by thy mighty power ; and grant that this day we fall into no sin, neither run into any kind of danger, but that all our doings may be ordered by thy governance, to do always that is righteous in thy sight, through Jesus Christ our Lord. Amen.

O Almighty God, the giver of every good and perfect gift, the fountain of all wisdom, enlighten, we beseech thee, our understandings by thy Holy Spirit, and grant, that whilst with all diligence and sincerity we apply ourselves to the attainment of human knowledge, we fail not constantly to strive after that wisdom which makes wise unto salvation ; that so, through thy mercy, we may daily be advanced both in learning and godliness, to the honor and praise of thy name, through Jesus Christ our Lord. Amen.

Our Father which art in Heaven, hallowed be thy name, thy Kingdom come, thy will be done in Earth as it is done in Heaven ; give us this day our daily bread ; and forgive us our trespasses as we forgive them that trespass against us ; and lead us not into temptation, but deliver us from evil, for thine is the kingdom, the power and the glory, for ever and ever. Amen.

II. AT THE CLOSE OF THE BUSINESS OF THE DAY.

Most merciful God, we yield thee our humble and hearty thanks, for thy fatherly care and preservation of us this day, and for the progress which thou hast enabled us to make in useful learning : we pray thee to imprint upon our minds whatever good instructions we have received, and to bless them to the advancement of our temporal and eternal welfare ; and pardon, we implore thee, all that thou hast seen amiss in our thoughts, words and actions. May thy good Providence still guide and keep us during the approaching interval of rest and relaxation, so that we may be thereby prepared to enter on the duties of the morrow with renewed vigor, both of body and mind ; and preserve us, we beseech thee, now and ever, both outwardly in our bodies and inwardly in our souls, for the sake of Jesus Christ, thy Son, our Lord. Amen.

Lighten our darkness, we beseech thee, O Lord ; and by thy great mercy, defend us from all perils and dangers of this night, for the love of thine only son, our Saviour, Jesus Christ. Amen.

Our Father which art in Heaven, hallowed be thy name, thy Kingdom come, thy will be done in Earth, as it is in Heaven; give us this day our daily bread; and forgive us our trespasses, as we forgive them that trespass against us; and lead us not into temptation, but deliver us from evil; for thine is the kingdom, the power, and the glory, for ever and ever. Amen.

The following forms of prayer, for the opening of schools, are taken from a very excellent volume of "Prayers for Schools," by N. Tillinghast, Esq., late principal of the Massachusetts State Normal School at Bridgewater;—a volume which will be found profitable for every teacher to study, if not convenient for him to use.

FORMS FOR MORNING PRAYER.

I.

We return humble and hearty thanks to thee, most merciful Father, that thou hast sent to us, through Jesus Christ, the revelation of thy law of love. Grant us the assistance of thy Holy Spirit that we may live in accordance with that law, loving one another, and doing good to one another as we have opportunity. We thank thee for that glorious liberty into which we have been called, by which a way is opened to us to escape from the slavery of sin, the destruction of that spirit which is the heir of an immortal hope. Grant that we may not make this liberty a cloak of licentiousness, but that, while we walk unbound, we may keep fast our dependence on thee, and look to thee, at every step, for guidance and support. Grant us, Almighty Father, clear notions of thee and of thine attributes; make us more humble, more sincere, more pure in heart; send us that wisdom which is from above, which is first pure, then peaceable, gentle, and easy to be entreated, full of mercy and good fruits, without partiality and without hypocrisy; and grant that this divine wisdom may be the man of our council, and the guide of our lives. Let thy blessing be with those for whom we should pray. May thy will be done in earth as it is in heaven, and may all men come to the knowledge and the love of thee, through Jesus Christ our Lord. Amen.

II.

Almighty Father, we know that thy listening ear is ever open to the petitions of thy creatures; that thou art more ready to hear, than we to speak; more ready to give, than we to ask; grant to us, we beseech thee, the spirit of prayer, that we may ask worthily that which we ought to ask at all; grant us faith, also, that we may pray with an entire confidence in thy mercy, believing that, whether we receive or not what we ask for, thou hast heard our prayer, and hast done what is best for us. We thank thee, that while we are pressed by a sense of our own weakness, and are surrounded on all sides by dangers beyond our control, we are called in thy gospel to look to thee, the Infinite Creator and Governor of all things, as our Father; may we keep this relation ever in our mind, and strive to do nothing unworthy of thy children; may our thoughts, words and actions, be kept in subjection to thy will. Amen.

III.

We humbly and devoutly thank thee, Almighty Father, that thou didst, in breathing into us the breath of life, create us in thine own image, with capacities to seek and to enjoy those things in which thou delightest. Thou hast surrounded us with trials and temptations, for in no other way than in resisting and overcoming these, can our moral faculties acquire strength. Assist us, we beseech thee, to carry on this conflict earnestly and steadily, looking to thee for help, and to him who was tempted like as we are, yet without sin, for guidance and example. Let no temptation beset us, that thou wilt not give us power to resist; may we not be overcome of evil, but overcome that evil in which we have heretofore lived with good. Thou knowest our peculiar weaknesses, and our peculiar wants; grant us help, we pray thee, Almighty Father, according to our respective needs; grant us the spirit of prayer, that whether in prosperity or adversity, in sorrow or gladness, we may ever turn to thee, and lay our thanks-givings or our petitions before thy throne. We entreat thee for thy mercy on all those with whom thou hast connected us in ties of kindred and affection; may the consolations of thy gospel be with all thy children; and may thy name be hallowed, and thy praise be sounded throughout all the earth; for thine is the kingdom, and the power, and the glory, now and forever. Amen.

IV.

Almighty Father, the giver of every good and perfect gift, in whom we live and move and have our being, in our ignorance and folly we come unto thee, the source of wisdom, and entreat of thee knowledge and understanding; grant us clear perceptions of truth, and a deep conviction of its infinite importance; may we feel that as no error nor deceit can exist in thy presence, so we may never hope to enjoy thy favor, if we train our minds to falsehood; may we learn and ever remember, that it is thy will that we should perform every duty, from the greatest to the least, with a perfect fidelity ; and grant us, we beseech thee, that single mindedness and that godly sincerity, that may enable us to give to every employment, and every situation, its just measure, so that nothing may appear to us as great or desirable which does not lead us forward in moral improvement, and nothing may seem to us mean or low which is useful to others, or profitable to ourselves. We thank thee, we render to thee our deepest gratitude, that we have ever before us a perfect model of how duty should be performed, in Jesus Christ ; he took upon himself the form of a servant, and was despised and rejected of men, that he might perform thy will, and satisfy his deep love of mankind by calling them to repentance ; may thy blessing be with us this day, leading us from evil, shielding us from danger, and bringing us nigher to thee ; and unto thy name, through Jesus Christ, or Saviour, be everlasting praises. Amen.

TOWN SUPERINTENDENTS.

RESOLUTIONS OF THE SCHOOL COMMITTEE OF BRISTOL.

At a meeting of the school committee held subsequent to the annual town meeting, it was *Resolved*, unanimously, to create the office of superintendent of schools ; and that the election of this officer shall be by ballot.

The following duties were assigned to the superintendent, and ordered to be published for the information of the citizens :

Resolved, That we do hereby create the office of superintendent, and assign to him the following duties :

1. The superintendent shall be secretary of the school committee. He shall keep the records, prepare all notices of meetings, and do all the writing and business incident to the committee.

2. He shall conduct the examination of teachers, giving notice of the time and place to the committee.

3. He shall visit and examine each school, at least once a month, and report the condition of the schools at each stated meeting of the committee.

4. He shall hold a meeting for teachers at least once a month, when opportunity shall be given for interchange of thoughts upon all subjects of discipline and study, and mode of communicating instruction.

5. He shall have a general supervision of the teachers, who, on all subjects connected with the discipline and conduct of the school, must submit to his decision, unless the same be reversed by the committee.

6. In every case of doubt or difficulty, the teacher may seek counsel of the superintendent. Whenever a pupil shall be very severely punished, or shall be expelled for misconduct, the teacher shall immediately report the case to the superintendent. He shall proceed to investigate the same ; and if the teacher, in his opinion, be justified, he shall explain the case to the parents or guardian of the offending pupil. But if he shall not consider the teacher justified, or if the said parents or guardian shall feel aggrieved by the decision, and desire an appeal to the committee, the superintendent shall call a meeting of the committee, and submit the case for their action.

7. It shall be his duty to respond to all applications for information respecting the schools, or the operation of the rules of the committee, and shall receive and notice all complaints, whether from parents, teachers or pupils.

8. He shall fix a time, (not less than one hour each school day,) when he may be seen for all purposes connected with his duties ; and shall cause notice of the same to be fixed at or near the entrance to his residence.

9. He shall receive, or cause to be received, under his responsibility, the assessments due quarterly from each pupil. He shall credit the amount received from each school, and compare the same with the whole number of pupils in said school ; and if there be a deficiency, shall ascertain and report the cause to the committee. He shall also record the names of pupils, who, on investigation, shall be found unable to pay their assessments, and shall furnish them with free tickets of admission.

10. He shall purchase, or cause to be purchased, under his responsibility, all books needed for the several departments, keeping on hand a number of each kind sufficient to meet the demand. He shall record the number and kind of books distributed to each school, that the same may be compared with the teacher's account of books received. All sums thus paid for books and stationery, shall be allowed by the committee out of the assessments, whenever the accounts, with the proper vouchers, shall have passed the auditing committee.

11. He shall see that all necessary repairs are made to the schoolhouse ; that they are cleaned at the close of each quarter ; that stoves are put in order and fuel provided, at the proper season ; that each school-room is in perfect order, and ready for occupation at the com-

mencement of each quarter. When the estimate of any expenditure thus made shall exceed twenty dollars, the subject shall be first laid before the committee.

12. All incidental expenses shall be made under his direction, and no bill, whether for salaries or incidental expenses, shall be paid by the treasurer, until examined and pronounced correct by the superintendent.

It shall be his duty to deduct from the salaries of teachers, such time as they may have lost from sickness or other causes.

All bills shall be paid as soon as possible after they have been incurred, and all accounts settled before the annual town meeting.

13. When a teacher, by sickness, or for any other reason, is prevented from attending school, such teacher shall cause notice to be given immediately to the superintendent, who shall provide, in the best possible way, for the continuation of the school.

14. He shall examine, on or before the last day of each quarter, all pupils in each school recommended by the principal of such school for admission to a school of higher grade; and his decision shall be final.

15. He shall examine all candidates for admission into the schools, from families removing into town, and all pupils not connected with any school the preceding quarter, and shall assign to them the particular school which they shall attend.

16. When families remove their residence to another place, the superintendent shall decide which school the children of such families shall attend. He shall also decide all similar questions connected with the limits assigned to each district.

17. He shall examine, in connection with the teachers, the pupils in each school, on the day of examination appointed by the committee. He shall, on the day of examination, furnish each teacher with a memorandum of the studies selected for examination, with the title of the book and page, and the time which shall be occupied in each.

18. He shall require from the principal of each school, a quarterly report in accordance with the rules of the committee. From these reports, he shall prepare an abstract in a book kept for reference, which shall always embrace the following particulars:

I. The number of pupils of both sexes.

II. The average attendance.

III. The names and number of pupils in the Delinquent Class.

IV. The branches of study pursued; the time daily devoted to each; with the number of pages studied in each text-book, and the number of classes.

V. The names of ten pupils in each school most distinguished for punctuality, good conduct, and attention to these studies.

VI. The number of times, if any, the teacher has been absent from school; or has been later in attendance than the hour prescribed by the committee.

VII. The instances, if any, where the rules of the committee have not been strictly observed.

VIII. The number of books furnished each school; the number and condition of all the books belonging to each school; the injury, if any, done to the school-house, or furniture; and the cause of the same.

19. He shall also make a quarterly report, recorded in a book for reference, giving a view of the progress of each school as compared with the preceding quarter, and embracing all matters and suggestions he may deem of importance.

20. He shall make an annual report, on or before the third Monday in March, embracing all the statistics of the schools for the year, the changes, improvements, or defects, that have been observed; practical suggestions for the future conduct of the schools; an account of his several duties and the time generally occupied in them.

21. These regulations shall comprise the duties of the superintendent until the same are altered by the school committee.

DECISIONS

OF

CASES UNDER THE SCHOOL LAWS.

—

It has been thought best, so far as possible, to collect all the late written decisions of the commissioners of public schools, and to print them in this edition of the law. They contain the commissioners' opinion on a variety of matters, and on the mode of interpreting the law ; and, of course, will serve as guides to trustees and school officers. These decisions, with a very few exceptions, have been made since the passage of the Revised School Law in 1851. The most important of them were made by the late commissioner, Hon. E. R. Potter, to whose deep interest in the subject of public education, it is in great part owing that the present law was enacted, and whose very intimate knowledge of the design and bearing of the law, eminently qualify him to give authoritative opinions concerning it. The decisions are given with a history of the case, with the belief that a statement of the circumstances attending each one, will be valuable to all who wish to make appeals.

A few decisions of the Supreme Court are also given, as establishing the views of the court on the powers and duties of school districts and their officers, and several opinions of his honor Chief Justice Ames, on the powers and jurisdiction of the commissioner of public schools. It is hoped that this publication will assist to interpret many points in the law, and therefore to aid in the vigorous enforcement of its provisions, and that it will tend to the improvement of our common schools, and the spread of intelligence among all classes of the community.

DECISION No. 1.

CASE OF SCHOOL DISTRICT NUMBER FIVE, CUMBERLAND.

1. School Teacher without a certificate cannot draw "teachers' money."
2. Irregular proceedings.

3. Mode of notifying meetings of the school committee.

In the case of the appeal of Albert Follet, of School District No. 5, Cumberland, it appears that,

In 1846, three trustees were elected. By misconstruction of the law, they supposed the trustees were to take turns acting year by year. In October, Follet was engaged and acted. The next year Scott, another trustee, acted, but there is no evidence of his being engaged. Crowningshield, the other trustee, removed from the district. But of these proceedings there is no record.

In May, 1848, a meeting was called by Scott, the clerk of the district, and who had also acted as trustee, and Mr. Follet, not an elector at the time, was chosen trustee, and engaged. But it does not appear that Scott was ever engaged either as clerk or trustee. The winter following, Mr. Follet employed Miss Burgess to keep the school. At the time she kept it, she had not any certificate, her former certificate from the committee being dated more than a year previous.

On December 16, 1848, a meeting of the school committee of the town was held; four members present, and the meeting was adjourned to December 19th, when seven out of nine members were present, one of the others being dead and the other sick. It is admitted that the meeting of the committee was not called according to one of their own by-laws, which provides that special meetings of the committee should be called by the secretary, on request, &c.

The committee voted that Follet was not the legal trustee of the district, and appointed an agent to establish a school there, and from this decision an appeal is made.

It is contended that this meeting was illegal, not being called in the mode pointed out in the by-law.

On the preceding facts I am of opinion,

1st. That no teacher can, under any circumstances, be entitled to demand any portion of the public money unless he has a certificate of qualification valid at the time he keeps the school.

2d. That the irregularity of the proceedings in the district has been so great, that the district cannot be considered as being legally organized.

3d. That although the committee may provide by by-law a mode of calling meetings of their body, such by-law would not exclude any other mode of calling meetings; and if a quorum be present, and all those who are capable of attending have had reasonable notice, and there is no charge of any unfair or improper proceedings, the meeting will be held to be a legal one ; the committee being a body appointed by law for performance of a trust, and the law itself prescribing no particular mode of calling such meetings.

E. R. POTTER, *Commissioner of Pub. Schools.*

Kingston, R. I., April 10, 1849.

Approved April 26, 1849.

R. W. GREENE, *Chief Justice Supreme Court.*

DECISION No. 2.

CASE OF SCHOOL DISTRICT NUMBER SEVEN, BURRILLVILLE.

1. A vote or decision of a school committee not involving the merits of a case may be appealed from.

2. School-house site fixed.

In the case of the appeal of sundry persons in School District No. 7, Burrillville, from a vote of the school committee of the town, passed second Monday of Jan., A. D. 1850, by which certain persons who had petitioned for a change of location of the school-house in said district, had leave to withdraw their petition because the committee were not fully satisfied that the petition came legally under their jurisdiction.

One question suggested but not argued on the hearing was as to the right to appeal from a decision of the nature above stated, not involving the merits of the question. I am of opinion, however, that the decision of the committee is such as may be appealed from, and that on such appeal the whole merits of the case may be examined and decided.

It appears that the district have always refused to accept a deed of the lot on which the school-house is now located, and that of course they have no legal title to the ground, and that the district owns a lot on the opposite side of the road from the old school-house on which the majority of the district are desirous to have the school-house stand.

From the above considerations and others presented, and believing that the peace of the district and the good of the school in the district would be promoted by a change of location, I do hereby change said location, and direct that the school-house be hereafter located on the lot conveyed by Mrs. Harris to said district, nearly opposite to where the old school-house stands.

E. R. POTTER, *Comm'r of Public Schools.*
Providence, Feb. 13, 1850.

The above decision is hereby approved.

LEVI HAILE, *Justice of the Supreme Court.*
Providence, May 30, 1850.

DECISION No. 3.

CASE OF SCHOOL DISTRICT NUMBER THREE, NORTH PROVIDENCE.

A school district ought not to be divided when it can conveniently establish a graded school.

In the case of the appeal of James S. Healey, Robert Newton and others, from a vote of the school committee of North Providence, passed Nov. 30, 1850, by which the School District No. 3, in said town, was divided into two districts.

It is contended on one side that under the proviso of sec. 4, p. 1, of the school act, the committee had no power to divide the district because schools of different grades might be conveniently established. It is admitted that there will be more than forty scholars in each of the new districts.

On consideration of the question I am of opinion that that portion of the proviso respecting the grading of schools, is to be construed as laying down a principle for the regulation of the discretion of the committee. It is not definite and positive in its terms, and cannot be made so from the nature of the case. Each case must depend upon its own circumstances. But before acting in such a case the committee should inquire and adjudge that each district will have the required number of scholars, and that the schools cannot conveniently be graded.

11

In regard to the facts of the case, taking all the circumstances together, and with the probability that the population of the north part of the district from its vicinity to the city must be constantly increasing, and that therefore the district presents a favorable opportunity of carrying out, sooner or later, the apparent intention of the proviso, I am of opinion that the district should not be divided, and the decision of the committee is therefore reversed.

E. R. POTTER, Comm'r of Public Schools.
Providence, April 16, 1851.

I hereby approve of the decision of the commissioner.

R. W. GREENE, Chief Justice Supreme Court.
April 18, 1851.

DECISION No. 4.

CASE OF SCHOOL DISTRICT NUMBER THREE NORTH PROVIDENCE.

1. School committee may not compel a gradation of schools.
2. Vote to establish a primary school.
3. School committee have power to limit and explain their certificates.
4. School committee cannot delegate its general powers.

In the case of the appeal of the trustees of School District, No. 3, in North Providence, from a vote of the school committee of said town, passed January 24, 1852, refusing to allow certain bills presented by said trustees, viz.: Anson H. Cole, for $48.12, for teaching school to January 8th, and Hannah T. Smith, for $18.00, for teaching school to January 23, 1852.

The parties were heard before the commissioner of public schools on Saturday, March 13, 1852; the trustees, Randall and Shepard, and Messrs. Sisson and Willard, chairman and clerk of the school committee, being present.

It appears, that by vote March 9, 1850, the school committee recommended the district to build or lease a room for a primary school, in the south part of the district,—that at a meeting of the district, August 6, 1851, the following resolution was offered:

"Resolved, That in the opinion of this meeting, the wants of the district imperatively demand the establishing of a primary school in the southerly part thereof; I move that a school-house for the use of the public schools of this town be built agreeably to the recommendation of the school committee of the town, the building of which school-house not to exceed $1,000."

And it was passed. A school-house was built.

Of the teachers employed, Mr. Cole had a general certificate, and Miss Smith a certificate for the primary school, near Corlis & Nightingale's, the new house being intended.

The trustees changed the teachers, and directed Mr. Cole to keep the school in the new house, and Miss Smith the school in the old school-house.

The chairman and clerk of the committee, by letter January 2, 1852, notified the t:ustees that the teachers should be restored to their former schools, and that unless the change was made on the following Monday, their bills would not be allowed. The change was not made, and when the bills were presented, the committee voted to allow only so much of them, viz. : ($43,75 to one teacher, and $3.60 to the other,) as was incurred before Monday, January 5th, "at which time the certificates of the said teachers were formally annulled."

It further appears, that the committee, by vote, October 18, 1851, authorized their chairman and clerk, severally, in the absence of the board, " to order bills, approve taxes, school regulations, &c., for the several school districts, and transact all other business legally transferable into their hands."

The appellants contend that the district schools had never been graded, that the committee had no power to grant conditional certificates, and that the committee had never legally annulled the certificates, (Sec. 14,) or dismissed the teachers, (Sec. 56.)

On full consideration of the points presented, and which were ably argued by Col. Rivers and Mr. Sherrod, for the trustees, and by Mr. Willard for the committee, I am of opinion,

1st. That the school committee may promote by advice and recommendation, but have no power to compel a gradation of schools by a district.

2d. That the vote of the district, (as explained by the vote of the committee, which is referred to in it, and thus made a part of it,) does appropriate the new house for a primary school.

3d. That the committee have the power to limit and explain their certificates. To construe the law to require perfection in the branches named in Sec. 54, would be unreasonable, and indeed, it is impossible to make a perfectly definite standard. If so, there is no reason why the certificate should not express the degree of qualification.

4th. That the committee cannot delegate their general powers. The powers of visiting schools and examining teachers they are spe-

cially authorized to delegate.*   There can be no objection, also, to a
committee authorizing its officers to draw orders for payment of bills,
upon the performance of certain conditions, as on making a return,
&c.   But to delegate a power, which is supposed to imply the exercise of a discretion in the committee, seems contrary to the intention
of the law in giving such power to the committee.

The committee have the undoubted right to annul a certificate, or
dismiss a teacher, for good cause.   No particular form is necessary
for doing this.   But the trustees should be plainly informed that the
certificate is annulled, or the teacher dismissed. And the teacher
should be notified, that he may have a chance to defend himself.

I see no reason, therefore, why Mr. Cole's bill should not be paid,
he having a general certificate ; and from considerations of equity,
and believing that the trustees did not consider that they were viola-
ting the law, or the lawful regulations of the committee, I think that
Miss Smith's bill, also, should be paid.

The town treasurer of the town of North Providence, is hereby
authorized and required to pay out of any money in his office standing to the credit of said district No. 3, (or if not apportioned, then
out of any school money in his office,) the sum of forty-eight dollars
and twelve cents, to Anson H. Cole, and the sum of eighteen
dollars to Miss Hannah T. Smith ; and in case the trustees have paid
the same, or either of them, then to pay it to said trustees, and for so
doing this shall be his sufficient warrant.

                                    E. R. POTTER, *Comm'r of Public Schools.*
Providence, March 23, 1852.

OPINION OF THE SUPREME COURT, GREENE, C. J.

The commissioner cannot draw orders on the town treasurers.

The following decision of the Supreme Court, made May 10, 1852,
relates to the Decision No. 4.   It will be seen on examination that it
only affects the mode of carrying into effect the decision of the commissioner of public schools in a case appealed to him :

---

* By the school law of 1839, the committee were expressly authorized to delegate
all their powers, and the practice was productive of great evil.

Mowry Randall and another vs. Zelotes Wetherell, town treasurer of North Providence.

Application for a mandamus. The application stated that the applicants, trustees of School District No. 3, of North Providence, "did on   day of   A. D. 1851, employ one Anson H. Cole, as teacher in said district, and that on the 8th of January, 1852, there was justly due to said Cole, as teacher, the sum of $18.12. That said trustees also employed one Hannah T. Smith, as a teacher in said district, and on the 23d of January, 1852, there was justly due to said Hannah, the sum of $18. That these bills were duly presented to the school committee of said town for payment, but said committee, January 21, 1852, by vote, refused to allow said bills, as they were by law bound to do, pretending that they were not due, and that the district was under no legal obligation to pay the same."

From this vote of the committee an appeal was taken to the commissioner of public schools, who decided that the bills should be paid and drew an order on the town treasurer to pay out of any money in his office, standing to the credit of said district, or out of any school money in his office, said sums to Anson H. Cole and Hannah T. Smith. This order the town treasurer refused to comply with.

A rule having been granted for the said Zelotes Wetherell to appear and show cause why said sums of money have not been paid, and why he should not be commanded by the court to pay the same.

Rivers for the petitioners cited sections 21st, 23d and 65th, of "an act to revise and amend the laws regulating public schools," and admitted that the statute gave the commissioner no direct authority to draw this order, but that the act having given an appeal from the town committee, who were competent to draw the order, the appeal to the commissioner carried with it by implication the incidental power to draw the order of payment.

The court having intimated that the proper mode of proceeding would have been for the commissioner to have certified their decision back to the town committee, and that upon their refusal to draw an order for the payment of the sums decided to be due, a mandamus might issue to compel them so to do. The further hearing of the case was postponed, that the court might ascertain the views which guided the school commissioner in his proceedings. The case was heard Saturday, May 8th; and now, the court having conferred with the school commissioner, their judgment was delivered by Greene, C.

J., (after stating the case.) The difficulty which the court experiences in this case, results from the 21st section of " the act to revise and amend the law regulating public schools," which defines the duties of the town committee. This section provides that the town committee shall draw orders upon the treasurer for the payment of money due, in conformity with the law: *Provided*, " that the committee shall not be obliged to give any order until they are satisfied the services have actually been performed for which the money is to be paid." They are to decide when money is due, and, having so decided, to draw an order for its payment. And the 23d section of the same act prescribes, that " the town treasurer shall receive the money due from the State treasury, and shall keep a separate account of all money appropriated by the State, or town, or otherwise, for public schools, and *shall pay the same to the order of the school committee*." These two sections are exceedingly significant. The first prescribes who shall draw the orders, and the other what orders the town treasurer shall be bound to pay. The 65th section of the school act gives an appeal from the decisions of the school committee to the commissioner, whose decision is to be final. But the commissioner, by this section, has only authority to affirm or reverse the decisions of the town committee, but has no authority to draw orders; and any orders drawn by him, are not obligatory upon the town treasurer. We think the proper course for him is to adjudicate upon the appeal, and certify his decision to the town committee, requesting them to draw the order required, and, if they refuse, a mandamus may be granted to compel them to draw the order.

Weeden for defendant.

DECISION No. 5.

CASE OF SCHOOL DISTRICT NUMBER THREE, NORTH PROVIDENCE.

1. Commissioner may rehear cases.
2. Former decision confirmed.

3. School committee to draw an order.

In the case of the appeal of the former trustees of said district from a vote of the school committee of the town, passed January 24, 1852, refusing to allow certain bills presented by said trustees.

This case was stated and decided by the commissioner on March 23, 1852, and an order directed to the town treasurer of North Providence, for the payment of the bills.

The Supreme Court subsequently decided that said order was illegal, and that the decision should have been certified to the school committee, for them to carry into effect.

On the 5th of June, 1852, a notice was issued to the school committtee to show cause why an order should not be made for them to carry into effect said decision; and on the 12th of June, Messrs. Sisson and Willard, on behalf of said committee, appeared and asked for a further hearing in the case, which was allowed—the old trustees objecting to the right to allow said rehearing.

The committee contend that the certificate of Cole, though general in its form, was by their practice limited to a grammar-school, and that this practice was generally understood; that the sub-committee had power to annul a certificate; that their letter did annul it, and that the whole committee subsequently approved it.

The other facts, points of law and arguments, are fully stated in the former decision.

On further consideration, I am of opinion that all the points of law before stated and decided were rightly decided; and further that the commissioner has a right to allow a rehearing for good cause, in his discretion; but so much of said decision as allows the bill of Miss Smith, is reconsidered and reversed, it not being in the power of the commissioner to dispense with the teachers' having a legal certificate.

And so much of said decision as relates to the bill of said Cole, is hereby confirmed, and the school committee of said town are hereby requested to draw an order on the town treasurer of said town for the payment thereof, being forty-eight dollars and twelve cents, to said Cole—or in case of said former trustees having paid the same to said Cole, then to said trustees.

E. R. POTTER, *Comm'r of Public Schools.*

Approved,   RICHARD W. GREENE, *C. J. Sup. Court.*

August 14, 1852.

DECISION No. 6.

CASE OF SCHOOL DISTRICT NUMBER SEVEN, BURRILLVILLE.

1. A district may rescind a vote order- ing a tax and postpone the payment of it.	2. A district may borrow money and give a note. 3. Costs of suits in court against a dis- trict must be paid by the district.

Office of Commissioner of Public Schools,
Providence, Oct. 25, 1853.

In the case of the appeal Syria Sherman and others, from a vote of the school committee of Burrillville, passed August 23, 1853, approving of the tax of $1,450, voted by District No. 7, in said town, for building a school-house and other expenses.

The question is presented whether a district having voted a tax according to a particular town valuation, can rescind the vote, postpone the payment, and hire the money upon a note of the district.

I cannot see any objection to the right of a district to rescind a vote ordering a tax and postpone the payment of it. The object and effect may sometimes be to include property and persons afterwards coming into the district. Whoever comes into a school district becomes a sharer in all the advantages of the school and district property. If by their coming, an addition to the school-house is made necessary, such new-comers or new property do not pay the whole expense of such addition: the former inhabitants and property have also to pay a portion, and sharing in all the advantages of former taxation, it does not seem unreasonable that the new property should also share in the burdens. In the present case the school-house was probably built larger than would have been necessary if it had not been expected that there would be an addition to the population of the district.

Any creditor of the district who may be injured by such postponement has a remedy provided by law.

As to giving notes, a district has the undoubted right to make contracts for certain purposes, upon which contracts they may be sued and the debt and interest recovered of them. A note given to such a contractor would be only additional evidence of his claim. And there seems to be no legal objection to the district hiring money of a third person to pay a just debt contracted for purposes authorized by law. This has been the construction always put upon the law in practice, and it appears to me sound.

An objection is also made to costs and attorney's fees. The costs of court in a suit decided against the district must of course be paid by the district. And the reasonable charges of an attorney for defending the suit are proper to be allowed. But services rendered by an attorney to any person in contests with other persons in the district about district business must be paid for by the person for whom they are performed.

Objection is also made to allowance of compound interest. This could not be recovered of the district at law, but I see no objection to the district's agreeing to pay it, and paying it if they see fit, as it would be in the power of the school committee to prevent any excess or abuse of the right.

I therefore confirm the vote of the committee approving of said tax.

E. R. POTTER, *Comm'r of Public Schools.*

DECISION No. 7.

CASE OF SCHOOL DISTRICT NUMBER THREE, NORTH PROVIDENCE.

1. School committee may limit their certificates, but general certificates must be construed to their plain purport.

2. School committee cannot delegate the power to annul a teacher's certificate.

Office of Commissioner of Public Schools,
Providence, January 8, 1853.

Appeal of Mowry Randall from certain votes of the School Committee of the town of North Providence, October 16, 1852, by which the bills of Anson H. Cole for keeping school in District No. 3, amounting to $122.50; Miss Hannah T. Smith's for $63; Miss Abby W. Thurber, for $31.50, were rejected.

After several adjournments, the case was heard at the office of the commissioner of public schools, December 18, 1852, the committee having been notified, and Messrs. Sisson, chairman, and Willard, of the committee, being present.

A part of the facts necessary to understand the case are stated in a former decision made March 23, 1842.

Mr. Cole had a certificate, general in its terms, and after the former decision continued to keep school in the same house, namely, the new or primary school-house.

The committee contended that the certificate of Cole, general in its terms, was by their practice limited to a grammar-school, and that this practice was made known to the trustees by the sub-committee's letter of January 2, 1852, if they had not known it before.

12

On consideration I adhere to the decision formerly made upon this point, that although the committee have the power to limit their certificates to particular schools, yet if they see fit to give a certificate of general qualification, it must be construed according to its plain purport, and to allow the written certificate to be contradicted or varied by any understanding not expressed on the face of the certificate itself, would be a dangerous practice, leading to continual misunderstanding and litigation.

But it is further contended that even if the certificate be a general one, and would allow Cole to keep in any grammar or primary school, that his certificate was annulled by the sub-committee's letter of January 2, 1852, and that if the sub-committee had not the power to annul it, the subsequent recognition of it by the committee annulled it.

In the former case, it was decided that the sub-committee had no authority to annul the certificate.

It is contended that the true grammatical construction of section 14 of the school law, authorizes the committee to delegate to a sub-committee the power of annulling certificates.

The power of annulling certificates is an important one. It gives the committee a control over the teacher—it authorizes them to pronounce a judgment against him for unfitness or misconduct, which may have the effect of ruining him in his profession, and of injuring materially his prospects for general success in life. If the construction was doubtful, these considerations would incline me to lean against the right claimed for the committee to delegate this power. But the construction appears to me to be plainly, that the committee have not the right to delegate.

And if the sub-committee had not the power to annul the certificate, the subsequent recognition of it by the committee would not render it valid.

In this view, it is not necessary to decide whether, if the sub-committee had the power claimed, their letter of January 2, 1852, would have been sufficient to annul the teachers' certificates.

Nor is it necessary to decide concerning Cole's former bill, as that has been settled since the appeal, and on the reconsideration which the committee ask, I cannot see any reason to change the opinions as to the law formerly expressed.

It being admitted that Miss Smith kept school in the house to which her certificate limited her, and her bill being rejected only on the ground that her certificate had been annulled at the same time and in the same manner as Mr. Cole's, this question is settled by the remarks already made.

As it is stated by the committee that Miss Thurbur's bill was postponed, not rejected, and that the certified copy presented from the records is in that instance incorrect, (by mistake, however, not by design,) no decision is made in relation to her bill at present.

The decision of the school committee of the town of North Providence respecting the aforesaid bills of Cole and Miss Smith, is hereby reversed and said bills allowed; and the said committee are requested to carry the decision hereby made into effect, and to draw an order upon the town treasurer of said town in favor of Anson H. Cole, for the sum of one hundred and twenty-two dollars and fifty cents, and an order in favor of Miss Hannah T. Smith, for the sum of sixty-three dollars, or in case the present or former trustees have paid either of said bills, then make the order for such bill in favor of the person so paying it.

E. R. POTTER, *Comm'r of Public Schools.*

DECISION No. 8.

CASE OF SCHOOL DISTRICT NUMBER THREE, NORTH PROVIDENCE.

A town superintendent of public schools must be appointed by the vote of the town, or by the school committee authorized by vote of the town to appoint.

Mowry Randall, of North Providence, former trustee of School District No. 3, appeals from a vote of the school committee of said town, passed January 15, 1853, rejecting the account of Miss Abby Thurbur, amounting to $31.50, for keeping school in District No. 3, of said town.

The school committee were duly notified, and after two postponements the case was heard before the commissioner of public schools at the state house in Providence, on the 19th March, 1853, the appellant and Messrs. Joseph T. Sisson, J. H. Willard and J. Mowry, of the committee, being present.

It appears that Miss Thurbur had a certificate, general in its form, and not limited to any particular school; that (there being more than one school-house in the district) she was notified by a sub-committee appointed by the school committee; that her certificate was annulled as soon as she began to keep in the old school-house; and that she did keep in said old school-house.

The sub-committee was appointed by the following vote, passed October 18, 1852 : " Voted, that in the absence of the board, the chairman and the secretary be severally authorized to order bills, approve taxes, school regulations, &c., for the several school districts, and transact all other business legally transferable into their hands," a copy of which vote is produced, certified by J. H. Willard, clerk of said committee.

Having decided in a case between the same parties, that the committee had no right to delegate the power to annul a certificate to a sub-committee, and that a recognition of it by the committee would not give validity to it, and having on request reconsidered the arguments, I see no reason for changing those opinions.

But on the hearing in this case, a new point is made, namely, that the sub-committee who annulled the certificate was a superintendent of schools, with all the powers of the committee under section 7 of the school law, and of course had full power to annul the certificate.

Section 7 of the school law is as follows : " Any town may appoint or authorize its school committee to appoint a superintendent of the schools of the town, to perform, under the advice and direction of the committee, such duties and exercise such powers as the committee may assign to him," &c.

It appears that the town, in town meeting, June 3, 1850, " voted that the school committee be authorized to appoint an agent to visit the schools, at a compensation not exceeding one hundred dollars, to be paid from the public school money," a copy of which is certified by the town clerk.

There is no evidence on record of the appointment of any agent or superintendent by the committee, but the certificate of the chairman (Joseph T. Sissom,) and clerk, John H. Willard,) is offered to prove that on the 18th October, 1851, (the same day on which the vote before recited delegating power to the chairman and clerk was passed) the following vote, or a vote in substance as follows, was also passed : " Voted, that John H. Willard be superintendent of the public schools of the town for the current year, with the privilege to employ, if necessary, suitable persons as substitutes, such services to be compensated from the residue of the appropriation of $100 voted last year by the town for such purpose."

Evidence to correct or supply omissions in the records of school officers I think may properly be admitted. In the case of clerks of districts, it seems absolutely necessary, as they are often unacquainted with the forms of doing business. In the case of a school committee, however, the presumption is stronger that they are competent men, and will be careful to see that their record is well kept. Yet even here great mischief might result from excluding all evidence other than the record. But it should be received with great caution, as after any considerable length of time, parties might not recollect it alike.

That a vote not recorded was passed at the meeting, is confirmed by the printed report of the committee for that year, in which Mr. Willard is spoken of as having been appointed agent at the preceding October meeting, with power to provide substitutes. The term used throughout the report, however, is *agent* and not superintendent.

On this state of facts the *first* question is, Did the vote of the town contemplate or authorize the committee to appoint a superintendent, such as is provided for by section 7 of the law? It seems plain to me that it did not, but that it meant only to provide for the visiting the schools, an important duty, but often neglected. The law authorizing the appointment of a superintendent was not passed until after this vote of the town.

As the committee must derive their authority from a vote of the town, it becomes unnecessary to notice further the proceedings of the committee. It may be proper, however, to observe, that the sub-committee who annulled the certificate did not style himself superintendent, and that if he actually had been superintendent his proceedings would not have needed any confirmation by the committee.

A considerable part of the difficulty appears to have arisen from mistake of the law, from not distinguishing between an agent to visit schools and a superintendent. If it was the intention of the town to authorize the committee to appoint a superintendent, and to delegate to him their whole powers; their vote should plainly say so.

The decision of said committee, rejecting said bill, is therefore reversed, and said bill allowed, and said committee are requested to carry this decision into effect, and to draw an order on the town treasurer of said town in favor of Miss Abby Thurber, for the sum of thirty-one dollars and fifty cents, or in case the present or former trustees, or either of them, have paid said bill, then to make the order for said bill in favor of the person so paying it.

E. R. POTTER, *Comm'r of Public Schools.*

Providence, June 8, 1853.

I approve of the above decision.

R. W. GREENE, *Chief Justice Supreme Court.*

DECISION No. 9.

CASE OF SCHOOL DISTRICT NUMBER TWELVE, BURRILLVILLE.

A vote of a school district to tax cannot be rescinded after a lawful contract has been made under it.

In the case of the application of Stephen A. Salisbury, late trustee of School District No. 12, of Burrillville, for the assessment and collection of a tax upon said district.

The parties were heard by the commissioner at a meeting at the district school-house, May 24, 1853, called by notice issued by the commissioner, and posted up on the door of the school-house.

It appears that at a district meeting legally notified and held on the 4th Dec., 1852, the district voted a tax of thirty-five dollars upon the property of the district in order to continue the district school three months, and the tax was subsequently approved by the committee of the town.

The trustee employed a teacher and commenced the school on the 13th December.

Jan. 4, 1853, several persons applied to the trustee to call a special meeting, and a notice was issued calling a meeting to be held Jan. 10. The meeting was applied for "for the purpose of considering the present tax, as there are persons taxed, who live and are taxed on the same property in another district; also property in the district not taxed." The notice also specified other objects, but no notice was given of any proposition to rescind the tax, nor did the request refer to any such intent, unless it is implied from the foregoing words.

At this meeting the district voted to rescind the tax and to direct the trustee to discontinue the school as soon as the public money was expended.

The trustee contends that he was authorized by the district to make the contract he did, and that the district had no right to rescind after the contract was made.

Under the old school law, if a district made a contract or authorized one to be made, and then refused to provide the means of fulfilling it, a suit might have been brought against the district in the State courts and damages and cost recovered against the district.

As this was expensive to both parties, the revised law, sec. 46, has provided in addition to the remedy by suit which still remains, that " if a district tax shall be voted, assessed, approved of, and a contract legally entered into under it, or such contract be legally entered into

without such vote, assessment or approval, and said district shall
thereafter neglect or refuse to proceed and collect a tax, the commissioner of public schools, after notice and hearing the parties, may
appoint assessors to assess a tax and issue a warrant to the collector
of the district, or to a collector by him appointed, authorizing and
requiring him to proceed and collect said tax." Under this section
the present application is made.

The fact of the tax being assessed, or of its having been approved
by the committee, would not take from the district the right to rescind
it. The whole turns upon the question whether a contract was legally
entered into under the vote of the district, and I am of opinion that
it was. The district therefore could not rescind it after the contract
was made, without being liable to a suit for damages or to a process
like that now applied for.

It becomes therefore unnecessary to decide whether the notice for
the second meeting was sufficient to justify the district in rescinding
the tax.

As a general rule, it is not advisable for district officers to proceed
in expending money or making a contract unless they are satisfied
that a majority of the tax-payers, absent as well as present, are fairly
in favor of it. A mere accidental majority occasioned by absence of
opponents is unsafe. And if a case should arise where district officers
should undertake to avail themselves of such an accidental majority,
and there should be any appearance of a design to anticipate or prevent a repeal of the tax by entering into a contract before there
could be time for having another meeting, the commissioner of public
schools would not lend the aid of his office to the enforcement of it,
but would leave the parties to their action at law.

In the present case, however, there is no evidence but that the
trustee acted fairly and honestly.

The proper process must therefore be issued for assessing and collecting the tax according to the before-mentioned provisions of the
law.

E. R. POTTER, *Comm'r of Public Schools.*

Providence, June 8, 1853.

I approve of the above decision.

R. W. GREENE, *Chief Justice Sup. Court.*

June 10, 1853.

DECISION No. 10.

CASE OF SCHOOL DISTRICT NUMBER TEN, NORTH KINGSTOWN.

School-house may not be used for any purpose other than for business directly connected with public education.

In the case of the appeal of Isaac Hall, of School District No. 10, of the town of North Kingstown, from the proceedings of the trustees of said district, in permitting the school-house in said district to be used for a debating society; the said trustees having been notified and heard before the commissioner at Wickford, on the 1st day of February, A. D. 1853.

The case involves the right of the district or trustees, to use the school-house for other purposes than an ordinary school, and depends partly upon the provisions of the general school laws, and partly upon the conditions of the deed of the lot upon which this particular school-house stands.

The following remark upon this subject is made in section 121 of the notes to the school act : "A school-house, built or bought by taxation on the property of the district, should not be used for any other purpose than keeping a school, or for purposes directly connected with education, except by the general consent of the tax-paying voters."

The rule here laid down is believed to be substantially correct and sound. The district holds the property in trust for educational purposes. The money has been taken from the tax-payers by force of law for certain purposes, and for those only, and cannot be applied by either district or trustee to any other use.

I am of opinion that under the school law the house may be used for educational purposes collateral to the main purpose, such as meetings of the district for school business, lectures upon literary or scientific subjects, debating societies for the people or children of the district, &c. It may not be easy in all cases to draw the line between legal and illegal cases, but it would be perfectly clear that the district could not use the house for trade or religious meetings, if any person objected to it.

The question then arises, whether the deed in the present case varies the rights of parties from what they would be if the deed contained no conditions.

By the deed from Joseph Case and others, dated October 11, 1848, the school-house lot is conveyed to the district "for the purpose of maintaining thereon a district school-house and appurtenances, for the benefit of the district school of said district, and for no other use or purpose whatever, except religious meetings," and it is provided " that when said lot of land shall cease to be occupied for the purposes of a district school aforesaid, the same shall revert to the grantors, their heirs and assigns forever."

The exception in regard to religious meetings may be left out of consideration in the present case. It cannot affect it in any way. If the district have no right to religious meetings there, independent of the deed, the deed cannot give it to them. And if the district would have such a right otherwise it may admit of question whether a provision in a deed would deprive them of it.

Leaving out of consideration the words, " except religious meetings," the remainder of the first passage quoted from the deed, appears to me, on the maturest reflection, to express no more and no less than the school law according to the construction herein given to it, would have expressed without the deed ; the provision in the deed is exactly in the spirit of the law, and neither adds to nor lessens the rights and powers of the district or trustees.

If the first passage quoted from the deed does not vary the rights of the district, from what they would be, if there was no such provisions in the deed, the latter proviso appears for the same reason to contain no limitation as to the use of the house, which would prevent its being used for the purposes for which I have said the law, apart from the deed, would authorize.

E. R. POTTER, Comm'r of Public Schools.

I have carefully considered of the above opinion and approve of the same. I have also consulted with Judges Haile and Brayton, who concur with me in opinion.

R. W. GREENE, Chief Justice Supreme Court.
March 4, 1853.

DECISION No. 11.

CASE OF APPEAL FROM SCHOOL COMMITTEE OF NORTH KINGSTOWN.

Scholars cannot be compelled to make fires for school-houses.

The regulation No. 26, adopted by the school committee October 25, 1852, is in these words : " The trustee or trustees of each district, with the teacher, may cause the fires to be made in the school-house,

13

by directing the scholars of a suitable age, to take turns in making the fires, or procure them to be made in any other way they may think proper."

In a private school the teacher has a right to prescribe his own terms. The parent who sends children to the school delegates to the teacher the right to govern them according to his own rules, and to punish to a reasonable extent for the violation of them. The remedy of the parent, if he does not like the school or its regulations, is in not sending to it.

Before the establishment of a public school system, all our schools were of this character. The practice of requiring the scholars to perform services of this sort, was generally adopted in the country schools, and in many of them has continued to this day. It remains to inquire what alteration the establishing of public schools by law, supported by the common funds and property of the State, has made in the rights of the parties in this respect.

To a public school every parent has a legal right to send his children. He sends them subject to the lawful authority of the teacher, and to the lawful regulations which may be prescribed for the discipline and studies of the school, but he has a right to insist that no regulations be made which the law does not authorize.

The right claimed, if it exists at all, must be derived from the general power of the committee to make regulations, or from the authority given to districts and trustees to make assessments on scholars and their parents. (Sec. 59.) The latter, however, it is very evident, contemplates only assessments to be paid in money and not labor.

The power of the committee to make regulations is given by section 16, which authorizes them, " to make and cause to be put up in each school-house, or furnished to each teacher, a general system of rules and regulations for the admission and attendance of pupils, the classification, studies, books, discipline and method of instruction in the public schools."

It seems to me very plain that the power to make a regulation of the character of the one in question is not given in this paragraph. We might as well infer a right to require the scholars to cut and saw the wood. And as I can find no other authority for it in the law, it must be considered as unauthorized by law, and accordingly null and void.

The practical difficulty in the case may be easily obviated by a voluntary arrangement on the part of the parents, or by making a small addition to the money assessments, and paying some person for attending to it under the direction of the teacher.

E. R. POTTER, *Comm'r of Public Schools.*

Providence, R. I., Jan. 1, 1853.

DECISION No. 12.

CASE OF SCHOOL DISTRICT NUMBER FIVE, LITTLE COMPTON.

A trustee of a school district can only be removed during his term of office for cause.

Office of Commissioner of Public Schools,
Providence, May 21, 1853.

From the best consideration I have been able to give to the subject, I am of opinion that a district having once legally made an election of any of the officers required by law to be elected, would have no right to rescind it.

The case would be different, however, with persons who were merely appointed by the district as a committee for some particular purpose. Over such cases the district would have complete control, and might remove such agents at pleasure.

A trustee once elected and accepting could only be removed for good cause and after notice and hearing. The contrary doctrine would lead to continual contests and confusion.

Very respectfully yours,

ELISHA R. POTTER.

DECISION No. 13.

CASE OF SCHOOL DISTRICT NUMBER THREE, NORTH PROVIDENCE.

1. A person who has the legal qualifications may vote in district meetings, even though his name is not on the town voting list.
2. A district has no right to build on a lot till it has a legal title to that lot.
3. The power to divide a district lies with the school committee.
4. A district should not make a contract to build till a lot has been secured.

Office of Commissioner of Public Schools,
Providence, October, 30, 1854.

In the case of the appeal of Stephen Randall and others, from a vote of the school committee of North Providence, relating to the location of a school-house in District No. 3, in said town, and from all the proceedings of said district in relation to a new school-house:

A hearing was appointed for October 10, 1854, and the clerk of the school committee and the clerk of the district notified thereof, and the hearing was then adjourned to October 14, 1854, when parties appeared and were heard for and against said appeal.

It appears that on June 26th, a district meeting was held, duly notified, when the district voted to build a new house, and procure a site for it, and also to raise up the West River school-house. At an adjourned meeting, July 5th, a tax was voted "sufficient but not to exceed the sum of $5,000 for the following purposes," viz.: to build the new house, to raise the West River house, to pay the debts of the district; and a committee was appointed to build and " otherwise do all such business required in the past sections of the warrant." At an adjourned meeting, July 17th, Eliza Angell having offered to give a lot to the district for a house " so long as it may be used for educational and religious purposes," a vote of thanks was passed. On July 31st, the district approved the plans of the house.

It appears that the committee made a contract for building on August 7th.

Application being made to the committee to approve the tax and plans, a meeting was held August 7th, and on August 28th, the committee approved of the tax, and also approved " the plan for school-house to be erected in District No. 3, a little south-east of the Wenscott House."

It appears from a certificate from Eliza Angell, that she could only convey the lot on the same condition on which her brother had conveyed the old lot on which a house had been built by subscription, viz.: for a public school-house, "and also as a place of public worship," and it was admitted that no deed had been made and the district had acquired no title to said lot.

It appears also from the statement and admissions of the parties, that a meeting duly notified was held August 17th, to reconsider all action relating to building the house, &c. At this meeting a motion was made to rescind the former proceedings, and, as declared by the moderator the vote stood 22 to 22, and the motion was declared rejected. It is admitted that five who voted for rescinding and five who voted against it, had no right to vote. It is contended that Asa M. Allen, who voted for rescinding, had no right to vote. He was a resident and owned real estate, and according to previous decisions he had a right to vote without his name being on the town registry. A certificate is produced from the assessors to show that Charles Leonard and Crawford Martin, two who voted against rescinding, are not taxed for real or personal property. Of course, not being liable to pay a portion of the tax, their votes should have been rejected. The vote, therefore, stands seventeen for rescinding and sixteen against rescinding, and the votes for building, &c., were legally rescinded.

This of course disposes of all questions relating to building, but the following points were made and argued, and therefore, to prevent further agitation, I give my opinion upon them.

I am of opinion that a district has no right to build upon a lot until they have acquired a legal title to it, either by lease, deed, or by taking it by process of law. And in the latter case, either the time for appeal to the common pleas should have elapsed or the appeal have been decided. The latter caution is necessary because the jury on appeal have a right to alter the location or wholly reverse all the proceedings.

It has been previously decided that a district has no right to take a deed of a house for religious purposes.

If the question of the propriety of dividing the district be proposed in district meeting, registry voters have a right to vote, because it merely amounts to an expression of opinion, and the whole power to divide rests with the school committee to whom the vote of the district is a mere recommendation to be weighed according to its deserts. And registry voters can by law vote upon all questions except taxing or expending money.

The proceedings of the district, and also of the committee in regard to the location, are not quite definite, but it is not necessary to consider them particularly.

It was also contended that the location must be made, a lot legally procured, and the plans approved before a contract can be legally made to build. In the present case the contract was made first. The question is in a most important one, because if a district proceeds before these things are done, it would often lead to a wasteful expenditure of the district's money if the lot was not procured or the proceedings approved of, and also because innocent parties who contract to build may suffer in consequence. In regard to claims of contractors against building committees or districts, those cases must of course be decided by the courts of law; but I think it is the duty of the school committees and school commissioner to guard against a wasteful expenditure of money by a district majority in all cases where they can do it, and it may frequently be in the power of the commissioner to do it on appeal. And it seems to me plain, (without undertaking to decide how innocent third parties may be affected by their acts,) that neither the district nor its officers have any right to make a contract until the lot is fixed and procured and the plans approved of.

The appeal was also made from all doings of the committee in relation to dividing the district; but I do not see any thing upon which the commissioner can act. The committee merely decided that the district had not asked to be divided. They did not reject the application. Any individual has a right to petition the committee for a division, and it would be matter of discretion in the committee to adopt or reject it.

E. R. POTTER, *Comm'r of Public Schools.*

— —

DECISION No. 11.

CASE OF SCHOOL DISTRICT NUMBER THREE, NORTH PROVIDENCE.

1. Qualification of voters in district meetings. | 2. Residence of voters.

Office of Commissioner of Public Schools,
Providence, December 23, 1854.

In the case of the appeal of Edward Finigin and Lewis E. Heaton, from a decision of the school committee of North Providence, by which their votes were excluded from the list of persons, who voted in a district meeting held in district No. 3, town of North Providence on the 17th of August, 1854:

A hearing was appointed for December 9, 1854; parties were notified thereof and appeared, and were heard for and against said appeal—and the case is as follows:

Several meetings, duly notified or adjourned, had been held in said district previous to August 17, 1854, at one of which it was voted to raise $5,000 for building a new school-house, raising one of the old houses, and paying the debts of the district. At another, it was voted to accept a lot offered on certain conditions by Eliza Angell, and to approve plans, &c., for the school-house. A meeting was subsequently held, after due notice, on August 17, 1854, to reconsider all previous action relating to the building, &c. At this meeting Walter Sharod presided; and a motion was made to rescind the former proceedings, and, as declared by the moderator, the vote stood twenty-two to twenty-two, and the motion was declared lost. No voting list being present, and there arising some doubt as to the legal qualifications of several who voted or claimed to vote, it was agreed by the moderator, and the parties at the meeting, to submit the list of the voters to the school committee of the town for examination and correction. The next day, therefore, this list was submitted to the committee, who, after examining and comparing the names of those who voted, as certified to them by the clerk of the district, with the town voting list, and striking off the names of those deemed not legally qualified—six who voted to rescind and six who voted not to rescind—declared that the vote on " the motion to rescind " stood yeas sixteen, nays sixteen, and that it was lost. Among those struck off or not counted, were Asa M. Allen, who voted to rescind, and Edward Finigin and Lewis Heaton, who voted against rescinding. Mr. Potter, the late commissioner of public schools, decided that the vote of A. M. Allen was legal, and should be counted in the affirmative, and that the votes of C. S. Leonard and C. Martin, which had been counted in the negative, were not legal, and should not have been counted ; and the result of his decision is, that there were seventeen votes in the affirmative, and sixteen in the negative. The question, therefore, turns upon the legality of the votes of Finigin and Heaton, which had been struck off by the school committee, and were not examined by Mr. Potter.

It appears in evidence that Finigin is a naturalized citizen, and a resident in said district ; that he has owned real estate sufficient to qualify him to vote since September 4, 1850 ; that his naturalization papers are dated March 4, 1851, and that he is taxable in the town, and is liable to be taxed in the district for the house in which he lives. It was contended that, his name not being on the town voting list, he could not, for this reason, be allowed to vote in district meetings. The qualifications for voting in district meetings are identical with those for voting in town meetings, with the same proviso as to voting upon any question of taxation. (See act relating to public schools, sec. 32.) But the restriction which forbids the moderator to receive the vote of any one whose name is not on the voting list, (see act relating to elections, sec. 26,) is not contained in the school laws, as a restriction to voting in district meetings. A moderator is therefore bound to receive and count the vote of a person who is a citizen and a holder of real estate in a district, whenever he has resided in it a sufficient length of time, even if his name is not on the voting list. Such is the opinion of the late commissioner of public schools, as expressed in his comments on the school law at paragraph 113, and also in his decision dated October 30, 1854, given on the case of Asa M. Allen, who claimed a right to have his vote restored, after it had been annulled by this same decision of the school committee.

In the case of Heaton, it is testified, that he became of age on the 28th of December, 1853, that he holds undivided real estate to a sufficient amount to qualify him to vote, and that he is a residens in said district. It is objected that, prior to August 17, 1854, he removed into Massachusetts, and thus lost his citizenship in Rhode Island. In opposition to this, it was proved that he went into Massachusetts for a merely temporary purpose, and that he never intended to change his abode, and that his estate, his business, and his real home, remained in Rhode Island. It appears to me that the principles which ought to govern in deciding questions of domicil or residence, as laid down by Judge Story in his Conflict of Laws, and quoted in Appendix No. 9 to the Report of the Commissioner of Public Schools for 1854, would render Heaton still a citizen and a voter in district meetings in Rhode Island, since his intention of only temporary removal seems plain.

It is, therefore, my opinion that the votes of Finigin and Heaton ought to be counted as against said motion to rescind. The vote will then stand seventeen ayes, eighteen nays; and the motion is lost. The several votes of the district relating to building are therefore still unrescinded, and of the same force and validity as if such motion had not been made.

No other points were made or argued in the case of this appeal, though I may add, there are several suggestions in the decision of the late commissioner, given October 30, 1854, which appear to me highly just, and deserving of the careful consideration of all concerned.

ROBERT ALLYN, *Comm'r of Public Schools.*

Approved.

GEO. A. BRAYTON, *Justice of the Supreme Court.*

December 30, 1854.

DECISION No. 15.

CASE OF LAYTON E. SEAMANS, A TEACHER DISMISSED BY THE SCHOOL COMMITTEE OF COVENTRY.

1. A teacher having a county certificate countersigned may be dismissed by school committee for cause.	2. A teacher, having been dismissed, cannot draw teachers' money.

In case of the appeal of Jason J. Potter, trustee of School District No. 5, of the town of Coventry, from a vote of the school committee of said town, whereby they refused to grant an order to pay the wages of Layton E. Seamans for teaching in said district; a hearing was appointed and took place April 21, 1855, in the village of Washington, in said Coventry, and the parties were heard. The following is a statement of the facts in the case as they appeared in evidence, namely:

It appears that the aforenamed Layton E. Seamans, applied, in October or November, 1854, to this school committee for examination as a teacher of a public school, and if that examination should be satisfactory, for a teacher's certificate of qualifications, to teach the winter school in the above-named District No. 5. The committee, however, as they had a legal right, and as they thought, upon their oaths they were bound to do, refused to examine him as to his literary qualifications, on the ground that they considered his moral qualifications insufficient for the requirements of the law. Mr. Seamans then succeeded in obtaining a county certificate from John H. Willard, Esq., a county inspector in Providence county, and also obtained the counter signature of the commissioner of public schools; both of these gentlemen supposing that no objections had ever been made to Seamans' moral character. With this certificate thus countersigned, Mr. Seamans entered the school in District No. 5, Coventry, as a teacher. He gave no notice of beginning to the school committee, neither did he in any way conform, or show a disposition to conform, to the rules of the said committee for the government or instruction of the schools of their town.

On the 26th of January, 1855, the committee formally dismissed him from his school, on account, as they alleged, of his having fraudulently procured the above-named county certificate, and non-compliance with their regulations.

Mr. Seamans, however, continued his school to the close of his term, when the school committee granted him an order for the money to pay his wages for the time previous to January 26th, 1855, and refused to grant an order for the time subsequent. It was from this refusal that the appeal was taken.

The commissioner is of opinion that the vote of the school committee, by which Mr. Seamans was dismissed, was a legal and proper vote, and in accordance with the 54th section of the act relating to Public Schools, which gives to a school committee the power to dismiss a teacher, by whomsoever examined, for just cause. The cause which they alleged appears to be a just and sufficient one. They had after this dismissal no right, according to the 21st section of the act above referred to, to grant any order to Mr. Seamans for services performed as a school teacher in any of the schools of the town, subsequent to the time when he was informed of the act of the school committee by which he was dismissed. The vote of the school committee is therefore affirmed.

Given under my hand at the office of Commissioner of Public Schools, in Providence, this 26th day of April, 1855.

ROBERT ALLYN, *Comm'r of Public Schools.*

DECISION No. 16.

CASE OF EMOR SMITH v. SCHOOL COMMITTEE OF SMITHFIELD.

Annulment of teacher's certificate.

Decision of commissioner of public schools in case of appeal of E. Smith, from a vote of the school committee of Smithfield, annulling the certificate of Smith as teacher in said town.

The vote from which this appeal is taken was passed by the school committee on the 29th day of January, 1855, and the appeal was received on the 3d day of February, 1855. Notice was given to the parties that the hearing would take place on the 10th of February, and on that day the case was opened and the testimony in part heard. The hearing was then continued from time to time by consent and agreement of parties, and finished on the 14th of July, 1855.

The facts necessary to a full understanding of the case, as they appeared in testimony, are briefly these : Some time in November, 1854, Emor Smith, of Glocester, was hired by Samuel Clarke, Esq., trustee of the twenty-first district, in Smithfield, to teach the winter school in that district ; and the bargain was, as is required by law, conditioned on Smith's obtaining a certificate of qualification from the school committee of the town. Smith called on Harvey Holmes, Esq., clerk of the school committee, to be examined, and not finding him at home, began his school on Monday, December 11, under a certificate given him the previous year, and still wanting a week of its time of expiration. On Friday, December 15, Holmes, in company with Dr. H. W. King, chairman of the committee, in compliance with the provision of the school law requiring the committee to visit each school within two weeks of its commencement, called upon Mr. Smith in his school, and found it in very great disorder. They were dissatisfied, according to their own testimony and that of Mr. Smith and scholars, with the ventilation of the room, with the mode of instruction and government, and with the general bearing and manner of the teacher. On Saturday, the 16th, the old certificate having expired, Mr. Smith called on Mr. Holmes and was examined, and finally obtained a certificate of qualifications, to be good for one year, unless sooner annulled. At the time of giving this certificate, doubts were expressed by Holmes in regard to Smith's ability to bring the school into order and properly to instruct it ; and it was finally concluded to give him the opportunity of four weeks' trial, at which time Holmes was again to visit the school. Accordingly on the 12th of January, 1855, Holmes visited the school again, and not finding any perceptible improvement, immediately sent a note to the trustee of the district, stating that he had annulled Smith's certificate. But no notice of the annulment appears to have been sent to Smith at all. Another teacher, however, was hired by the trustee. Smith appealed to the commissioner of public schools, and a partial hearing took place on the 27th of January; and on the 31st, the committee failing to appear, the act of Holmes was decided to be void, since in fact no annulment had been made, nothing but a notice having been sent to the trustee that such annulment was made.

The school committee of Smithfield, however, met on the 29th of January, and by a unanimous vote proceeded to annul the certificate of said Smith, given him by Harvey Holmes, and dated Dec. 16, 1854, "for deficiency and want of qualification." It is from this vote that the appeal is taken, and in reference to this that the following decisions are made.

The first point made by the Hon. J. M. Blake, council for Smith, was that the decision reversing the act of Holmes, made on the 31st of January, necessarily was conclusive in this, and reversed it also. That, however, was clearly an illegal act done by a single member of the committee, to whom no such power to annul was ever delegated,—in fact, there is no evidence to show that Holmes ever wrote an annulment. He undoubtedly supposed that he had annulled the certificate of Smith, but the contrary is clear; and therefore the committee were at liberty to take original action in the case. It is their act that is to be examined on its own merits. And this can only be justified where it is shown that the circumstances of the case actually called for this course on their part.

A second point made for the appellant was, that he had no notice of the intention of the committee to annul his certificate, and therefore he had no opportunity for trial and defence. It is believed, on this point, that the conversation which passed between him and the examiner was notification enough that he was to have four weeks for trial and practical demonstration of his ability to teach and to govern in the school-room. And this is a better form and mode of trial than can be had elsewhere. It is therefore decided that such a trial is sufficient, especially as the teacher always has an appeal, where it can be examined whether the trial in the school was fair and sufficient.

The points made by A. Meggett, Esq., council for the committee, were two.

1. That Smith was not qualified in literary attainments for the office of teacher; and,

2. That he failed to comply with the regulations for the schools of Smithfield made by the school committee, and that he failed to impart instruction and to govern in a proper manner his school.

On the first of these points, the commissioner does not feel bound to go back of the certificate of the committee. They, or their clerk, gave him a certificate in proper form, under their oath, after due examination and consideration of the circumstances. It must, therefore, be held that he was qualified, at least to make trial of his skill in the school-room.

The case, then, must turn wholly on the questions, whether or not Smith did comply with the regulations of the school committee, and whether he did really properly instruct and govern his school. The testimony on this point was large in amount and conflicting in character. But these facts appear clearly to be proved by the testimony of the school committee, the affidavits of two visitors, by the statement of Smith himself, and by the affidavits of scholars. That there was a great amount of noise and confusion in the school-room; that scholars were allowed to whisper; that the room was not well ventilated, and that the modes of punishment were not proper; all of which were in direct violation of the regulations for schools, posted by the committee on the wall of the school-room; and further, that Smith himself was boisterous and rough in his manner, and not only neglected to give information and assistance to his scholars when asked, but that he allowed the scholars to miscall or mispronounce words in their reading lessons without correction; and, in general, that the scholars did not improve, and were nearly losing their time and making a waste of the public money.

These being the facts in the case, as appears to the commissioner of public schools, it seems to him that the school committee of Smithfield only discharged the duty imposed upon them by the law and by their oath of office, and their act of annulling the certificate of the said Smith ought to be sustained. And said act is accordingly hereby affirmed; and the certificate of qualification as teacher in the common or public schools of Smithfield, given by Harvey Holmes, clerk of the school committee of said town, to Emor Smith, of Glocester, and dated Dec. 16, 1854, is declared to be annulled from and after Jan. 29, 1855.

Given under my hand, at the office of Commissioner of Public Schools, this 24th day of August, 1855.

ROBERT ALLYN, *Comm'r of Public Schools.*

This decision was, by request of the parties, submitted to Chief Justice Staples, and on Sept. 26, (Wednesday,) the annexed note was received from him, and at his request is appended.   R. A.

Robert Allyn, Commissioner of Public Schools :

DEAR SIR,—I have attentively examined your decision in the appeal of Emor Smith against the school committee of Smithfield.

As a general rule, a teacher ought to have an opportunity to be heard before his certificate of qualifications is annulled. Such a certificate confers on him the right to be employed as a teacher of a public school. The annulling of it takes from him that right. When, therefore, proceedings are commenced with a view to this result, he ought to have notice to appear to show cause against it.

His want of success in teaching or governing a particular school may be a sufficient reason for annulling the certificate of a teacher, if it arise solely from his deficiency. But it ought not to be taken for granted that the teacher can neither explain nor excuse nor justify such apparent want of success. It would seem but common justice to allow him an opportunity to do so.

Upon the facts contained in your report and decision, I see no reason to disapprove of it, made as it was after notice to Smith, and after hearing all that he had to offer in denial, excuse or justification of the facts alleged against him.

Very respectfully your ob't serv't,

W. R. STAPLES, *Chief Justice Sup. Court.*

Wednesday morning.

DECISION No. 17.

PETITION OF EMOR SMITH FOR REHEARING.

Rehearing not possible after approval by a judge of the supreme court.

Office of Commissioner of Public Schools,
Providence, Oct. 18, 1856.

Opinion in the matter of the petition of Emor Smith for a rehearing of the decision of the commissioner of public schools, on his appeal from the school committee of Smithfield.

Upon reading and considering this motion and petition for a rehearing, it appearing that the matter of said appeal had been decided by me as commissioner of public schools, and that a statement of facts, at the request of the petitioner Smith, was by me laid before Hon. William R. Staples, late chief justice of the supreme court, and was by him approved,—all which facts are recited in said petition,—I hereby decide to dismiss this motion and petition for reconsideration of said decision, upon the ground that the approval of the decision in said appeal by Judge Staples being made by law final, I have no power or jurisdiction to rehear or reconsider the same.

Given under my hand the above day, Oct. 18, 1856.

ROBERT ALLYN, *Comm'r of Public Schools.*

OPINION OF HIS HONOR CHIEF JUSTICE AMES.

Jurisdiction and duties of the Commissioner of Public Schools.

In the matter of the decision of the commissioner of public schools in case of the appeal of Emor Smith from a vote of the school committee of Smithfield annulling the certificate of said Smith as a teacher in said town.

This is a motion or petition for a reconsideration by the commissioner and the judge of the above decision, on the ground that the decision of the commissioner reported to the Hon. William R. Staples, late chief justice of the supreme court, on the 24th day of August, 1855, and approved on the 26th day of September, 1855, is not valid and binding, because the commissioner did not report a statement of the facts as they were sworn to or admitted, but instead thereof reported *as facts* his own conclusions upon the testimony; it appearing from the petition of said Smith that "he insists that there can be no final or binding decision, until *a statement of the evidence* shall be made to the judge," for reasons by him in his petition set forth.

The 65th section of the "act to revise and amend the laws regulating Public Schools," provides, "that the commissioner may (and if requested on the hearing of either party shall) lay a statement of the facts of the case before some one of the judges of the supreme court, whose approval of such decision shall be final." If, then, in the matter of this decision, upon such request, a statement of the facts of this case, in the sense of the statute, has been laid before one of the judges of the supreme court, and the decision of the commissioner has been by him approved, this "approval" is, by the very words of the statute, made final, irrespective of the merits of the decision approved. The "appeal," in other words, in the civil law sense of the term, and as it is used in our statutes, that is, a rehearing of the whole cause, matter of fact as well as law, after it has been decided by a competent tribunal, is expressly given by the first words of the section of the school act above referred to, to the commissioner; and the section provides that his decision upon such appeal shall be final, if the commissioner, upon the request of either party, shall "lay a statement of the facts of the case" before one of the judges of the supreme court, and he shall approve the decision. The purpose of this last provision was, undoubtedly, to give to the commissioner and the parties the aid of such a judicial officer in matters of law, and to secure, as far as conveniently practicable, by an uniform construction of the act, an uniform system of legislation upon so important and interesting a subject as the discipline and government of our public schools.

The document annexed, entitled "Decision of commissioner of public schools in case of appeal of E. Smith from a vote of the school committee of Smithfield annulling the certificate of Smith as teacher in said town," signed by Robert Allyn, commissioner of public schools, with Judge Staples' note to the commissioner subjoined, approving of the commissioner's decision, with the original petition of Emor Smith to Rev. Robert Allyn, commissioner of public schools: "In the matter of Emor Smith's appeal from the school committee of Smithfield, embracing forty-one pages, together with the decision of the said Robert Allyn hereunto prefixed, dismissing this motion or petition for reconsideration for want of jurisdiction, have been laid before me, according to the request contained in said petition, by the said Robert Allen as commissioner, for my approval, and I do hereby approve of his dismissal of said motion or petition, on the ground that he has no jurisdiction to entertain the same."

The document entitled "Decision, &c.," is, in my judgment, "*a statement of facts*" by the commissioner in the sense of the 65th section of the school act, although it is not, as it is averred by the petitioner that it is not, a statement of the testimony or evidence by means of which the commissioner ascertained the facts which he states in it. "A statement of facts" from testimony or evidence must, from its very nature, be the conclusions of the officer entitled to make it, from the testimony or evidence which he has heard; and the distinction between such a statement and a statement of the evidence or testimony upon which it is based, is too well settled in legal practice and parlance to require illustration. Whether the conclusions drawn from the evidence or testimony by the commissioner were legitimate or not, is a matter which the law does not, in my judgment, confide to the judge, but solely to the commissioner, who alone hears the appeal, listens to the witnesses, examines the evidence, and arrives at the conclusion of what are "*the facts of the case.*" No power, no means, are, in my judgment, given to the judge to examine into these facts. It is the duty of the commissioner, under the law, to decide what the facts are, and to lay a statement of them before the judge, with his decision upon them, and the sole office and jurisdiction of the judge is, upon such statement, to approve or disapprove the decision of the commissioner. This is not only plain from the words of the act, but is to be inferred from the nature of the facts to be ascertained, the good or ill discipline of schools, the fitness or unfitness of teachers to instruct or discipline scholars, and the like facts, peculiarly fitted to be ascertained from evidence by the commissioner, but which the judge would ordinarily have no such peculiar qualifications to ascertain.

The jurisdiction of courts and judicial officers over visitors of collegiate or academic bodies, whether at the common law, or as measured out by statutes, is ordinarily of the most limited character, both in England and in this country, and for the very reason, that, beside the fact that the visitor is presumed to be selected by the founder or the State as best fitted to judge in matters of collegiate or academic discipline, his power is, as said by Lord Mansfield in the celebrated case of The King v. The Bishop of Ely, (1 Wm. Blacks. Rep. 82,) "certainly very convenient for these learned bodies. It is *forum domesticum,* calculated to determine *sine strepitu* all disputes that arise within themselves; and the exercise of it is in no instance more convenient than in that of elections. If the learning, morals or proprietary qualifications of students were determinable at common law, and subject to the same reviews as in legal actions, there would be the utmost confusion and uncertainty; while he who has the right may possibly be kept out of the profits of what is in itself but a temporary subsistence.'

Accordingly, upon subjects within his jurisdiction, it is the well settled doctrine of the general law in England that the sentence of a visitor is final and conclusive; nor can the King's Court, in any form of proceeding, either directly or collaterally, review the sentence. The action of the courts in such cases is confined to inhibiting him from proceeding beyond his jurisdiction, taking care, where the general matter is within his jurisdiction, not to anticipate his own judgment as to his jurisdiction to do the particular act which he is called upon to perform. It has even been held, that, where a visitor has actually executed a sentence of expulsion, though he may appear to have exceeded his jurisdiction, a mandamus will not lie to restore the party expelled; for that would be to command a visitor to reverse his own sentence. See Angell and Ames on Corporations, 5th ed., sec. 693, pages 750, 751, and cases cited. And where, as is sometimes the case in this country, power is given by charter or legislative act over the sentence of visitors, it will be found to be confined to matters of law—such as, Have they acted contrary to the statutes of the foundation, or, Have they exceeded the limits of their jurisdiction? As an instance, see Murdock's Appeal, 7 Pick. 320, 321.

The jurisdiction of the school commissioner under the public school act, by way of appeal from the decisions or doings of school committees, district meetings, trustees and county inspectors, is, looking to the subject, nature and manner of its exercise, rather a visitatorial power, than that of an ordinary legal tribunal,—and the power of the judge of the supreme court in the matter of such an appeal is limited, precisely as might have been anticipated from the universal course in such cases,—to the mere approval of the decision of the commissioner upon his statement of the facts.

It being admitted by the petitioner in his said petition that the decision and statement of facts of the commissioner in the matter of this appeal was laid by the commissioner before Chief Justice Staples on the 24th of August, 1855, and that the said decision was, by said Chief Justice Staples, then one of the judges of the supreme court, approved,—and it appearing to me that the statement of facts submitted to said judge, was such a statement of facts as is required by the statute, and that his approval thereupon of the decision of the commissioner is final,—I therefore approve the decision of the commissioner, that this motion or petition for reconsideration must be by him dismissed for want of any jurisdiction in him alone or in him conjointly with a judge of the supreme court, to rehear or reconsider the decision so approved.

After such a decision and approval made, neither the commissioner nor Judge Staples, if the latter were still in office, could rehear or reconsider the matter of the same, no matter how erroneous such decision and approval might be. Much less can the commissioner, with another judge of the supreme court, or subject to approval of such judge, whether then in office or succeeding to the office of Judge Staples, reconsider and rejudge his approval.

SAMUEL AMES, *Chief Justice Supreme Court of R. I., &c.*

Providence, October, 20, 1856.

DECISION No. 18.

QUESTIONS BY JOHN H. CROSS, ESQ., OF SCHOOL DISTRICT NUMBER ONE, WESTERLY.

1. Tax may be voted, but cannot be collected without the approval of the school committee.
2. Rate bills approved by the school committee will remain in force till specially repealed.
3. Every district meeting has a right to adopt its own rules of order, and the moderator can only vote as other voters do.

Office of Commissioner of Public Schools,
Providence, June 22, 1855.

No. 1. "Is a district authorized to lay or collect a tax without the approval of the school committee?"

Answer. I think a district may vote to "lay" or levy a tax,—indeed, as the district must first act, it is necessary that they shall so vote, before the school committee can approve. The district cannot collect a tax which has not been approved by the school committee. But Mr. Potter has decided, in case of District No. 14, Smithfield, and his decision was approved by Judge Greene, that "although it is prudent to procure a tax to be approved by the school committee before any legal proceedings are had under the vote, yet it is sufficient if the tax be approved before the warrant is issued to collect it." Your second query is similar to this, and my reply to that will finish this point.

No. 2. "Has any vote of a tax by a district any legal force, until approved by the school committee?"

Answer. I think not, so far as the law is to be used in collecting it. But it may be said to have legal force in a certain sense before the school committee approve or disapprove. The collector cannot have legal authority to collect it till approved, and hence it cannot be a tax in the full legal sense without the approval of the school committee.

No. 3. "If a district has voted to support its schools, by rate bills or tuition fees, and has fixed the rates within the limits prescribed by the school law, and the school committee has approved the vote and the rates, and if said district should afterwards vote to support the schools entirely by a tax upon the ratable property of the district, would not the former vote continue in force until the latter shall be approved by the school committee?"

Answer. In case of a district which had established a rate bill which had been approved by the school committee and did not repeal this rate bill at the time of voting to support its schools by tax, I am of opinion that the approved rate bills would remain in force in case the committee should disapprove of the tax on the property, and I think they could be legally collected. In case the district had voted to abolish the rate bills, that vote would of course hold good without the approval of the school committee. The only point of doubt is as to whether a vote to support schools by a tax on property necessarily repeals a rate bill before the school committee approves. I ought not to decide this very difficult matter without argument heard in the specific case. But I incline to think it does not so repeal a rate bill until the committee approve, after that approval of course the rate bill is repealed.

No. 4. " Has not a district which has adopted no special rules of order, the legal right to reconsider a vote passed at any previous meeting, whether adjourned or dissolved, and will not its action directly upon the reconsidered vote be valid ?"

Answer. Our school law makes every district a corporate and not a legislative body. It may therefore adopt its own rules of order. And the law is not very particular as to any prescribed forms. Every motion or every point of order raised in a district meeting would be debatable, and I think from a little reading that all points of order should be settled by vote. The law gives to the moderator of a district meeting no authority to decide points of order, nor to give a casting vote. He can only vote on the same conditions as the other citizens of the district vote. This point of order, then, must be decided by vote, and all such votes, however unparliamentary in legislative bodies, would, I think, be valid.

Yours, &c.,
ROBERT ALLYN, *Comm'r of Public Schools.*

DECISION No. 19.

CASE OF JOHNSON AND CARD *vs.* SCHOOL COMMITTEE OF WEST GREENWICH.

A teacher without a certificate of qualification cannot draw public money.

Office of Commissioner of Public Schools, }
Providence, April, 21, 1855. }

In case of the appeal of Ezekiel T. Johnson and George L. Card, teachers of public schools in West Greenwich, from a vote of the school committee of said town, by which vote the said committee refused to grant them orders for their wages in consequence of their, the said Johnson and Card, not having been examined, the commissioner of public schools is of opinion that the vote of said school committee was in strict accordance with the letter of the school law, and said vote is hereby affirmed.

ROBERT ALLYN, *Comm'r of Public Schools.*

DECISION No. 20.

CASE OF SCHOOL DISTRICT NUMBER EIGHT, NORTH PROVIDENCE.

Commissioner cannot compel trustees to grant a warrant for the collection of a tax, and must not interfere to perform their duties.

Decision upon the petition of sundry tax-payers in School District No. 8, North Providence, asking for the collection of balance of tax levied in said district.

The case presented is as follows: A tax was voted November 21, 1852, for building a school-house in School District No. 8, of North Providence. It was also voted to borrow the money with which to build, and the amount to pay, both principal and interest, was ordered to be assessed upon the ratable property of the district according to the next town valuation. The money was borrowed, the tax assessed and partly collected; and the commissioner is now asked to appoint a collector and to issue a warrant to collect the balance.

The hearing was appointed for September 3d, and was then adjourned to the 6th, at which time Messrs. Hayes and Jencks appeared as counsel for George M. Richmond, a tax-payer in said district opposed to the granting the petition, and raised a question of jurisdiction, and moved that the petition be dismissed because the commissioner had not power to grant the relief prayed for. The point was argued by Hayes and Jencks, for the objectors, and J. H. Willard, for the petitioners.

After consideration the commissioner submits the following as his decision on the question of jurisdiction:

It is seriously doubted whether, under the forty-sixth section of the school law,—the section cited as giving all the authority over the case,—the commissioner has power to order and enforce the collection of the balance of a tax legally voted, approved, assessed, and partly collected by a district under the rightful authority of their trustees. The case contemplated by that section appears to be one in which there is no power in the district to collect taxes and thus satisfy any just claims which creditors may have against it ; and not one in which the power has already been exercised to a certain extent, and the officers of the district are simply indisposed to proceed. The petition does not allege any errors in the assessment nor any want of power to collect, but only asks the commissioner to perform a duty legally devolving upon their officers, but very repugnant to their feelings ; or, in other words, it is but asking one officer of the State to undertake a duty where his authority is at least doubtful, and discharge it for another where the latter's power is far more clear.

Besides, it seems that according to the sixty-sixth section of the school law, the trustees of the district have a right to presume that the tax was a legal one, and that it is, therefore, properly and lawfully due, inasmuch as there appears to have been no exception taken to the vote by which it was ordered, nor to the act by which it was assessed.

It is a principle which must govern the commissioner, that he will not encroach upon the powers, prerogatives or duties of any officer below him elected by the people themselves. And as the trustees of the district were elected for this very purpose of collecting all lawful taxes, and as they have ample powers and securities, the petition is therefore dismissed.

ROBERT ALLYN, *Comm'r of Public Schools.*

Office of Commissioner of Public Schools,
Providence, September 10, 1855.

DECISION No. 21.

CASE OF JOHN H. WILLARD *vs.* TRUSTEES OF SCHOOL DISTRICT NUMBER TWO, NORTH PROVIDENCE.

The legal school year begins May 1st, annually.

Decision in case of the appeal of John H. Willard from a decision of the trustees of School District No. 2, in the town of North Providence.

This case was heard by the commissioner of public schools at his office in Providence, on the 15th of September, and is as follows :

It appears that the appellant, John H. Willard, has been employed for several years as principal of the grammar-school department kept in School District No. 2, of the town of North Providence. For the last two years, his salary has been, at first, fifty dollars per month, then fifty-five, and at last sixty, if there should be a remainder of the public or "teachers' money" sufficient to pay him that amount, after paying the other teachers in the district; and on this salary last named of sixty dollars per month, he was teaching at the time of the last annual meeting, held on the 29th of May, 1855. At this annual meeting the election of trustees for the ensuing year was made, and Jesse S. Thornton, Amos M. Read and Andrew Almy were chosen. They entered upon the duties of their office. Mr. Willard continued in the school as teacher, and received, under the authority of these trustees, two months' wages, at sixty dollars per month. At the close of these two months the summer term of the school ended, and there was a vacation till the first or second Monday in September. During this vacation, and about a week before its close, and the beginning of the fall term, the trustees, through Mr. Almy, one of their number, informed Mr. Willard that they had decided to reduce his salary from sixty to fifty dollars per month, or, in the event of his not accepting that price, to dismiss him from his place as teacher in their school. It is from this decision of the trustees that the appeal is taken.

The facts were all substantially agreed to by the parties; that Mr. Willard's salary had been raised as above stated from fifty to sixty dollars, partly in consideration of the fact that the funds of the district had been sufficient, and because of the increased cost of living, and partly also in consideration of a long time of "good and faithful services" in the school; that the teachers employed in the school had been hired with no definite stipulations as to the time of their continuance in school, but with a general mutual understanding that they were to continue throughout the year, and longer, if neither party gave notice to dissolve the connection; and that the teachers now engaged in the school had been employed for several terms,— one for several years,—during which time nothing had been said, neither at the beginning nor end of the school terms, about a new engagement, but that they entered upon new terms as though they were employed permanently.

The trustees, by themselves and Mr. J. T. Sisson, urged in justification of their course, that the funds of the district properly denominated "teachers' money," were insufficient to pay more than fifty dollars per month to the principal of the grammar department; that they have always reckoned their school year to begin in September, at the beginning of the fall term, and that of course the contracts with their teachers were all, at that time, subject to renewal, modification or termination; and that they have such control of the affairs of the school that they can in general dismiss a teacher or make a change in the amount of his salary at their own pleasure.

On the other hand it was contended by Mr. Willard that the amount of money apportioned to this district by the school committee of the town, and called "teachers' money," was amply sufficient to pay him nearly sixty dollars per month, and that the agreement with the trustees was such that they would be compelled to pay him only so much as might be in their treasury if it should fall short of the sixty; and in evidence of this the account-book of the school committee was introduced, which showed one thousand three hundred and forty dollars and forty-eight cents ($1,340.48,) standing to the credit of the district, while the monthly expenses for teachers' wages and board—reckoning Willard's at sixty—would be one hundred and thirty-one ($131,) and this for ten and one-half months (10 1-2,) would be one thousand three hundred and seventy-five dollars ($1,375.) (This estimate and calculation will be the same at whatever time the year is made to cominence.) On this point he also suggested that, by the school law and according to a rule of the committee, any unexpended balance remaining to the credit of the district at the end of the school year must be divided among the other districts of the town. He also contended that the legal school year terminated and commenced at the time of the annual meeting in April or May, according to the statute creating districts to be corporations, with strictly defined and limited powers, and that therefore as he had received, under the authority and by the order of these trustees two months pay of the present year; that he was now engaged under a virtual renewal of the contract of the year, which contract could only be changed by mutual consent of parties or for cause, according to the school law.

The commissioner is of opinion that the money subject to the trustees' order is very nearly sufficient to pay the amount of sixty dollars as named in the agreement between Mr. Willard and the trustees of last year, but he must say that he thinks this question should have no influence whatever upon the final decision. And besides that, at the proper time of the year, and under the approbation of the school committee, the trustees have unlimited authority to employ a teacher at whatever wages they please. If they employ at very high wages, they may, under the approval of the committee, collect limited rate bills; or, by a vote of the district, they may assess and collect a tax to defray the extra expense. If they employ at cheap wages, the unexpended balance of their appropriation must be divided among the other districts. And if trustees choose to use only a part of their share of the "teachers' money," for their own district, and leave the remainder to other districts, thereby providing an inferior school for their own children and a better one for their neighbors', no power is known to prevent, provided they do it at the proper time. At such times as trustees may lawfully hire teachers for their schools, they may hire as cheaply as they can, provided the school committee will approbate those hired. It may not always be enlightened policy to employ at as small wages as possible, but under the circumstances just named, there is no remedy.

In reference to the time when the legal school year commences, there can be but one opinion. In absence of any vote of the district prescribing the time at which the teachers' contracts shall terminate, and in the absence of any written or specific agreement between the trustees and teachers as to this time of terminating the contracts, and in such districts as have established permanent or yearly schools with fixed terms and vacations, the legal school year must be settled by the statute. Section 21 of the act relating to public schools, makes it necessary for a district to keep a school not less than four months at some time during the year ending on the first of May, in order that it may be entitled to draw its portion of the "teachers' money" for the year thereafter ensuing; the commissioner is required by section 2, annually in May to apportion the money annually paid out of the general treasury for public schools among the several towns, according to law, and his office annually expires on the second Tuesday of that month. Section 20 enacts among other things that the school committee " shall apportion as early as practicable in each year, among the districts, the money received from the State;" and section 21 further provides "that at the end of the school year any money which shall remain unexpended may be divided by the committee among the districts the following year;" and finally, section 26 makes it the imperative duty of a district to hold its annual meeting near this time, namely in April or May. From all this and from the fact that the returns of the districts to the school committees and from the committees to the commissioner are made to this date, and the school district officers are elected for the year ending at their annual meeting, and expire then, unless continued by special statute, the commissioner must decide that the legal school year begins on the first of May annually, or by section 26, in cases there provided for, at the time of the annual district meeting, and in the absence of all proof of any specific vote of the district, or of any specific agreement between the trustees and Mr. Willard, that the contract for salary was from the time of the annual meeting held on May 29th, 1855; and that the payment of two months salary after that time was a virtual renewal of the agreement for another year, and should so be held in common justice and honesty, unless for reasons good and sufficient, the school committee of the town should dismiss him, as they have a right to do under the 56th section of the school law.

As to the general power claimed by the trustees to reduce a teacher's wages, or, in the alternative, to dismiss him from their school, and that on a very brief notice, it should be remarked, that the school law manifestly intends that the State shall have some charge of all the schools which it in part supports. It therefore very properly forbids trustees to hire as teachers persons who do not possess certain moral and literary qualifications,—and even those who possess these in an undoubted degree, unless they hold or can obtain a certificate in the required form and signed by the proper authorities. The law aims to prevent trustees from retaining a teacher who neglects his duty, and provides that the school committee may dismiss such an one. It also evidently contemplates making the office of teacher one of dignity and permanence, for the certificate has an existence of from one to three years, according to the signature it bears. All these guards seem to be reared in order to prevent the trustees of a school district from doing two things which would necessarily tend to destroy or degrade their school: from employing the immoral or incompetent, and thus poisoning or stinting the morals and the minds of the children, and from hastily dismissing the worthy teacher by reason of any private or personal pique, or in consequence of some temporary excitement. And as the State furnishes a portion of the money which supports the public school of every district, and gives that district all the right it has to exist, and to collect taxes for the further support of its schools, it is but proper that it should step in by its officers and prevent the trustees from injuring the school, or from suddenly discharging or reducing the compensation of a teacher against whom no deficiencies are alleged. It is believed that such powers as are claimed would materially injure any school, and that under the school law they are not conferred upon the trustees.

The commissioner of public schools therefore declares that the aforenamed decision of the trustees is reversed, and he affirms Mr. Willard's right to teach as principal of the grammar department of the school in District No. 2, of North Providence, at the same salary

16

per month as he has had for the first two months of the current year.

Give at the office of commissioner of public schools, in Providence, this 22d day of September, 1855.

ROBERT ALLYN, *Comm'r of Public Schools.*

DECISION No. 22.

CASE OF EDWARD S. WILKINSON, GUARDIAN, IN APPEAL FROM TAX IN DISTRICT NUMBER ONE, NORTH PROVIDENCE.

1. Imperfection of a district clerk's record does not render invalid a tax properly voted.
2. Commissioner will not decide that a vote to assess by percentage is illegal.
3. The assessment of a tax will be legal if it is clear to whom and on what property it is assessed.
4. Taxes must be assessed to a ward in the district where the said ward actually resides.

This case was heard at the office of commissioner of public schools, on the 1st day of April, 1856, and the facts, as submitted in evidence, and agreed to by the parties, are as follows, namely :

Edward S. Wilkinson, the appellant, a citizen of North Providence, and a resident in School District No. 2, in that town, is guardian of Nathan Lazelle, a minor. The said minor has, since his father's decease, boarded in the family of a lady whose residence was for several years in the same district, No. 2, with Mr. Wilkinson. More than a year ago, she removed within the limits of School District No. 1, and the said Nathan still continued to board with her in her new residence. The family of this lady is admitted to have been the usual home of this minor, although he has for several months during each of several years, been absent in other places attending schools for the purposes of education.

On the 8th day of October, 1855, the trustees of School District No. 1, above named, Hiram Cleveland, M. D., Olney Arnold, Esq., and A. R. Franklin, Esq., by printed notice posted up, called a special meeting of the legal voters of the district, to be held on the 12th of that month, for the purpose of voting a tax to pay the debts of the district, and doing any other lawful business. This meeting was accordingly held on the above named 12th of October, and a vote was passed levying a tax of twenty cents on the hundred dollars, for the purpose above specified in the warrant calling the meeting.

This tax was assessed by the trustees before mentioned, and by the town assessor, as is provided in the act relating to public schools. As the trustees found Nathan Lazelle, a minor, boarding, and, as they supposed, residing within the bounds of their district, No. 1, and possessing personal property, they assessed a portion of this tax to him— putting it upon the district tax-book, as it was upon the town tax-book, to " Edward S. Wilkinson for Nathan Lazelle."

It is from this vote of the district, at the said special meeting, by which this tax was ordered to be assessed and collected, and also from the act of the trustees in assessing that tax, that the appeal is taken. And it is alleged that the records of the district clerk are imperfect, and do not show that the said meeting was legally notified, nor that the resolution ordering the tax specified the purpose for which the tax was levied ; and that the act regulating the assessing and collecting taxes requires that a vote to tax shall specify the sum to be levied, while this only specifies the rate or the per cent. ; and further, that a tax could not lawfully be collected of Mr. Wilkinson for Lazelle, unless it specify the relation, whether guardian, trustee, or otherwise, of said Wilkinson to said Lazelle ; that said minor could be taxed only where his guardian resided ; and finally, that taxes had been paid for the said minor in Wilkinson's own district, No. 2.

On the other hand, it was shown by proof that the imperfection above alluded to, was in the records alone, and not in the proceedings of the meeting, that the notice was legal, and that the resolutions and votes were in proper and legal form—if the mode of levying by percentage instead of by specific sum alone be excepted ; and that the tax was assessed to " E. S. Wilkinson for N. Lazelle," as had been previously and commonly done by the town.

Upon these facts, and after considering the arguments of the parties, and after advising with Judge Brayton, of the supreme court, the commissioner is of opinion that the imperfection of the records of the clerk will not affect the legality of the tax. The proceedings, so far as the notice of the meeting and the form of the resolution are concerned, were undoubtedly legal and proper. As to the mode of levying the tax by percentage instead of by specific sum, the commissioner is not aware that this is contrary to the school law. It is evident that the school committee might approve a specific sum after the tax had been assessed by the trustees ; and as there is no evidence to show that the committee did not approve some specific sum, it must be held that the failure to vote a specific sum, does not render the whole tax invalid. Also in reference to the assessment of the tax to Edward S. Wilkinson for Nathan Lazelle, instead of to Edward S. Wilkinson, guardian for Nathan Lazelle, since it was shown that this had been the mode of assessing taxes on the said Nathan's personal property in the town of North Providence, and since it was not shown that the said Wilkinson had ever experienced any difficulty in the settlement of his accounts with the said Nathan's inheritance before the court of probate, the commissioner does not deem it to be proper for him to interfere, and solely on this account decree a forfeiture of the tax on the part of the district. This is a matter of technical law and he does not therefore attempt to settle the meaning and usage of that law. It is deemed just and best that in this case, this tax should follow and be paid as other taxes have been paid.

As to the question of residence, there is no testimony to show that this ward, Nathan Lazelle, was ever at any time considered, either by himself, by his guardian or by others, a member of his guardian's family; but on the contrary there is much to induce the inference that he has always considered his home with the lady in whose house and family he was boarding at the time the tax was assessed. Such being the case, the said Lazelle should be regarded as a member of her family; and if he continued to board with her in her changed location, he would be liable to taxation for his personal property in the school district where she resided.

The act of the trustees is, therefore, sustained, and the tax against Edward S. Wilkinson, for Nathan Lazelle, is hereby affirmed.

Given at the office of commissioner of public schools, this 15th day of June, 1856.

ROBERT ALLYN, *Comm'r of Public Schools.*

DECISION No. 23.

CASE OF SCHOOL DISTRICT NUMBER EIGHT, WEST GREENWICH.

District trustees must act as a board.

Meetings of Trustees of School Districts and their Duties.

Decision in case of appeal of Greene and Wood, citizens and trustees of District No. 9, West Greenwich.

An appeal was sent to the commissioner of public schools, signed by Caleb Greene and Jonathan N. Wood, from West Greenwich, and received at the office on the 15th of November, 1855, appealing from the action of Joseph Nichols, Esq., a trustee of School District No. 9, in said West Greenwich, who in connection with the citizens of said district hired a teacher for the winter school of said district.

The facts on which this appeal is based, as they appeared in evidence taken at the trial which was held in the school-house in School District No. 9, on the 21st of November, 1855, are as follows : Joseph Nichols, one of the three trustees of said district, made a contract with Layton E. Seamans, of Coventry, on the 11th day of October, 1855, under the following circumstances : Instead of calling a meeting of the three trustees, he called a meeting of the citizens of the district at the school-house, and laid before them the terms of the contract which it was proposed to make with Seamans. It appears that there was at this meeting a discussion as to the probability of Seamans being able to draw the public money on account of his State certificate having been annulled ; and after the discussion it was very generally agreed—only one man decidedly objecting—to hire Mr. S. on the proposed terms. Several, however, expressed doubt, but concluded to make no objection, and among these was Jonathan N. Wood, another trustee of the district, who thus gave at least a qualified assent to the arrangement. The other trustee, Caleb Greene, was not present at the meeting. It also appears that this meeting of the voters of the district was not called legally, but only informally, and that the trustees were not notified to meet as trustees.

The question is as to the legality of a contract thus made.

And here it is proper to say that immediately after the trial a mutual arrangement was made between the appellants and Mr. Nichols, by which the school was to go on, and a new contract was made according to the terms of the law by the trustees, so that the question is now only purely abstract, and relates solely to the proper mode of calling meetings of trustees of school districts, and to the method of conducting business in these meetings.

The commissioner, therefore, decides that a district, at a meeting of its voters, has no power to hire a teacher even if the meeting is legally called, and such an item is inserted in the warrant. In sects. 33–36, inclusive, of the act relating to public schools, which enumerate the powers of districts, no mention is made of the " power to employ " teachers ; but, on the contrary, sec. 40, specially confers upon the trustees that power, and it is made " their duty " " to employ one or more qualified teachers for every fifty scholars in average daily attendance." It is, therefore, the plain duty of the trustees to employ all teachers, and a meeting of the voters of a district could only be advisory.

As to the mode in which the trustees shall discharge their duty, it ought to be a rule never to be departed from, that when the district appoints three trustees, as it may, the three should meet and confer upon all questions relating to their official duty. Many of their duties are deliberative, and, therefore, cannot be delegated to, or assumed by, any one of their number; such as making contracts with teachers, or for repairs or fuel, preparing tax lists and rate bills; and these things, of course, require a meeting of the three, or at least of a majority after due notice given to the absent minority. And it is highly improper, that any single one should, in any duty not strictly ministerial and prescribed to him by vote of the body at a meeting, act with the expectation that his colleagues will ratify what he shall have done.

The mode of notifying meetings of trustees is not specified by law, and is therefore left to be a matter of common agreement among them. Generally, as they are near each other, a verbal notice from the chairman will be sufficient.

Given under my hand, at the office of commissioner of public schools, in Providence, this 20th day of February, 1856.

ROBERT ALLYN, *Comm'r of Public Schools.*

June 16, 1856.
Approved.

GEO. A. BRAYTON, *Associate Justice of the Supreme Court.*

DECISION No. 24.

CASE OF SCHOOL DISTRICT NUMBER THREE, NORTH PROVIDENCE.

All business of special meetings of school districts must be specified in the notice of the meeting.

Decision in case of Walter Sherrod and William E. Dodge, on appeal from vote of School District No. 3, North Providence.

This appeal was from a vote of a special meeting of District No. 3, North Providence, held on February 15, 1856, at which time Philip B. Stiness, Jr., was elected trustee of said district, in place of John Trainer, who had previously sent in a letter resigning his office. The hearing was appointed for February 28, at 12, M., at the office of the commissioner of public schools; at which time and place the parties appeared before the commissioner, and the following are the facts in the history of the case, as they were proved or admitted by the parties, viz. :

At the annual meeting of the district, held May 31, 1855, Walter Sherrod, William E. Dodge, and John Trainer were elected trustees of the district for one year. Some time during the month of September, 1855, Trainer, in writing, communicated to the clerk of the district, his resignation of the office of trustee. On the 1st day of February, 1856, a notice, signed only by Sherrod and Dodge, the two acting trustees, was put in the proper places, calling " a special meeting " of the legal voters of the said district, (No. 3,) at the school-house, on Wednesday, the 6th day of February, at 7, P. M. " To receive the new school-house, order bills, and do any other business that may lawfully come before said meeting." The meeting was accordingly held, and after other business had been done as named in the notice, inquiry was made respecting a rumored resignation of Trainer. The clerk presented such a letter. A motion was then made to accept the resignation, and it was immediately concluded to postpone taking the question on that motion to the adjourned meeting, which was ordered by vote to be on the 15th of February, at 7 P. M.

At the fixed time the adjourned meeting took place. This was a continuation of the former meeting held under the same warrant, for the same purposes and for none other. At this meeting it was voted to accept the resignation of Trainer, and immediately thereupon it was voted to proceed to fill the vacancy so caused. Philip B. Stiness, Jr., and Joseph Healey were nominated, a ballot was taken, and, after counting, the moderator declared Stiness elected, he having a majority of all the votes cast.

It is from the vote thus declared that the appeal is taken, and it is claimed that the school law imperatively requires that the business of every special meeting shall be named in the warrant by which it is called; wherefore the commissioner is asked to declare the election of Stiness null and void, and he is requested to lay a statement of the facts and of his decision before one of the judges of the supreme court for his approval.

The commissioner is of opinion that such an election cannot be considered valid. Section 29, of the school law enacts, that notice of the time, place, and *object*, of every special meeting shall be given for five days inclusive, before the holding of the same. The notice put up on the 1st for a meeting to be held on the 6th, contained no specification concerning the election of a trustee; and as this meeting was adjourned, and another notice was posted up, it must be held, that the meeting of the 15th was not competent to elect a trustee—an item of business not named in the original warrant. If it is said that a motion was made to accept the resignation of Trainer, and this being postponed to the next meeting was a sufficient notice of the intention to elect a trustee, it will be an ample reply to say, that such postponement cannot be considered a notice according to the requirements of the law. For section 30 of the school law specifies the mode of notice, which is " by publishing in some newspaper, or by putting up notice, or in such manner as the school committee may require." The notice certainly was not given in any of these three ways. It may also be said, that if the law requires the business of every special meeting to be named in the warrant, trustees, if so disposed, might prevent action on any necessary matter by failing or refusing to insert it as an item in the warrant calling the meeting. But section twenty-seven, of the school law, provides against this by commanding the trustees to call a meeting " within seven days, on the written request of any five qualified voters, stating the object for which they wish it called," and if the trustees neglect or refuse to call such meeting, the school committee may call it and fix the time of holding it. The election of a trustee was therefore not proper business to come before the meeting, either of the 6th or the 15th of February, and the election of Philip B. Stiness, Jr., is hereby declared void.

Given at the office of commissioner of public schools, in Providence, this fifteenth day of April, 1856.

ROBERT ALLYN, *Comm'r of Public Schools.*

July 1, 1856.
Approved.

GEO. A. BRAYTON, *Associate Justice Supreme Court.*

DECISION No. 25.

CASE OF SCHOOL DISTRICT NUMBER THREE, WEST GREENWICH.

Decision of commissioner of public schools in case of appeal of Charles Andrew, from the vote of the school committee of West Greenwich, by which they refused a portion of the public money to School District No. 3, in said town.

This appeal was made to the commissioner of public schools on the 12th day of April, 1856, and heard at his office in Providence, on the 29th of the same month, and, by adjournment, was continued to May 1, 1856. The history of the case, and the facts as they appeared in evidence, are as follows:

The general assembly at its October session in East Greenwich, in 1854, passed an act in relation to School District No. 3, West Greenwich, to allow said district to draw the public money and use it to support a school in a school-house owned by proprietors, and standing on the north side of the stream running through the district, until the first of October, 1855, and until they should build a school-house on or near Carr's corner, on the south side of the above-mentioned stream; and the same act appears to have contemplated compelling—though without a penalty—the building of this new school-house.

Immediately after the passage of this act, the district held a legally notified meeting and voted to build the contemplated school-house on Carr's corner, and appointed a building committee of three to procure plans and specifications, to purchase and take a deed of the lot, to make contracts for the school-house, and to superintend its erection. This building committee, understanding that the location of the house was fixed by the act of the general assembly, procured plans and specifications and laid them before the school committee for approval as the law directs. The committee retained these plans and finally failed to act, either by way of approving or disapproving. Two of the building committee soon after their election resigned, and two others were appointed by the district in their places, and this latter building committee has taken no action in reference to the new school-house. In these circumstances, as the committee of the town did not approve, and the committee of the district did not act, and since the new school-house could therefore not be built as contemplated by the act of the general assembly, the trustee of the district continued the school in the proprietor's school-house on the north side of the stream, and applied to the school committee of the town for their district's portion of the public money to pay the teacher's wages. The school committee, by vote passed at their regular meeting on the 2d day of April, 1856, refused to grant an order for any portion of the public money, alleging that said proprietors' school-house was, by the before-named act of October, 1854, to cease from and after October, 1855, to draw any portion of the public money. It is from this vote, passed under these circumstances, and for these reasons, that the appeal is taken.

An appeal is also taken from the act of the school committee, and from the usage of the town in dividing the money received from the State treasury and from the town tax equally among the districts in the town, and it is alleged that the school law obliges every town to apportion the money so received from the State, one-half of the town's

17

portion of $35,000 equally among the districts, and the other half in proportion to the average attendance of scholars in the schools of the several districts.

And the school committee ask that the commissioner of public schools shall lay his decision before one of the judges of the supreme court for his approval.

In reference to the vote of the school committee by which they refused to grant any portion of the public money to School District No. 3, since October, 1855, the commissioner is clearly of opinion that the act upon which they claim to ground their refusal, can bear but one construction, namely : that the public money shall be paid to support the public schools kept in the proprietors' school-house on the north side of the stream, until October, 1855, and till the contemplated new school-house is built on or near Carr's corner. The district appears to have attempted in good faith to carry out the design of the act of the general assembly to build a school-house, and to this end they passed the necessary votes and elected a building committee. This committee also appears in good faith to have submitted plans and specifications of a school-house to the town's committee as the law requires, and by the failure of this committee to act they were prevented entirely from accomplishing their design. Had the town's committee disapproved these plans, an appeal might have been taken and their decision could have been reversed. But as they neglected to act, the intention of the district was completely frustrated, without any fault on its part. The committee of the town may have acted and probably did act without intention to frustrate the design of the law ; but it neglected its plain duty in the case, and if the statute cited were even different from what it plainly is, it ought not to take advantage of its own negligence to deprive one district of its just portion of the public money and to divide that portion among the other districts of the town.

It was at the time of the trial contended that the building committee ought, by the act referred to, and by the school law, to have carried their plans to the commissioner of public schools for approval. But the act of October, 1854, only specifies that the commissioner, in the event of a non-agreement of the district to build on the lot specified on Carr's corner, shall " locate the said school-house," and the general laws command that every school-house shall be built after plans approved by the school committee of the town or the commissioner of public schools. The building committee then ought first to apply to the school committee of the town, and in case of their disapproval or refusal to act, they could then carry the plans by appeal or otherwise to the commissioner. But by the neglect of the committee in this case, and by their retaining the plans, the building committee were totally prevented from carrying them to the commissioner, who properly has no original jurisdiction in such matters.

The commissioner, therefore, decides that School District No. 3, is justly and legally entitled to the balance of its true proportion of the public school or teachers' money, and the said vote of the school committee of West Greenwich is hereby declared to be reversed; and the said committee are hereby commanded to draw an order on the town treasurer of said West Greenwich for the said balance, viz.: fifty-one dollars and seventy-three cents ($51.73) now due to said district.

In reference to the second part of said appeal, which asks that the commissioner would reverse the act of the committee of said town dividing the public school money equally among all the districts of the town, the commissioner decides that he can afford no relief. The general school law does indeed expressly state that the one-half of the money given from the general treasury for public schools in any town shall be divided in proportion to the average attendance of scholars in the several schools of the town; and the other half equally among the several districts. But it does not specify the manner in which a town may divide the money raised by its own vote, and that arising from the payment of registry and military taxes. It was given as the opinion of the late commissioner, Hon. E. R. Potter, that towns are at liberty to divide this according to their own pleasure, so that they use it judiciously for the good of their schools. It may follow, therefore, that a town may so divide its own money and registry and military taxes as to make up the inequalities in the sums payable to its several districts, that would arise from the legal division of the State's money. And as the usage is of long standing thus to equalize the portions of public money paid to the several districts in West Greenwich, the commissioner sees no reason to disturb it, and feels that he has no authority so to do; and further, it does not appear that this district, No. 3, is deprived of any money it would have had under the division of the public money according to the technical language of the statute.

Given at the office of commissioner of public schools, in Providence, this nineteenth day of May, A. D. 1856.

ROBERT ALLYN, *Comm'r of Public Schools.*

June 16, 1856.

Approved.

GEO. A. BRAYTON, *Associate Justice Supreme Court.*

DECISION No. 26.

CASE OF SCHOOL DISTRICT NUMBER SEVEN, BURRILLVILLE.

No person to vote on any proposition to raise a tax, unless he is liable to pay a part of said tax.

Decision of commissioner of public schools in case of appeal of Daniel S. Mowry and others from certain votes declared to be passed at certain meetings of the voters of School District No. 7, Burrillville, held on March 29, 1856, and continued by adjournment to May 12, 1856, and also on the first Monday in May, 1856.

This appeal was received at the office of the commissioner on May 10, 1856, and the time of hearing was fixed for the 22d of May, at which time the parties appeared and the case was continued to June 12, 1856, when it was heard, and the following are the facts as they were substantially agreed to by the parties, namely:

In 1853, a tax was assessed in District No. 7, Burrillville, for the purpose of building a school-house, or paying for a school-house then lately built. A part of this tax was collected, namely, the sums respectively assessed to Smith Aldrich, $10.01; A. Bowen and wife, $6.93; Stephen Clark, $21.56; Jos. O. Clarke and wife, $43.11; Walter T. Harris and mother, $2.31; P. W. Hawkins & Co., $15.40; Alvah and Russell Mowry, $10.78; Alvah Mowry, $12.70; D. S. Mowry, $22.01; Phebe Mowry, $2.31; D. Smith, Jr., $21.56; S. Wood, $29.25; O. Youngs, $26.94; S. H. Youngs, $1.54; S. A. Aplin, $1.54, amounting in all to $229.95. This tax was, when these sums had been collected, declared by the late commissioner of public schools to be illegal, and the tax was ordered to be reässessed in February, 1854. Of this reässessment, the above sums were counted as paid, and the following sums were paid additional, namely, the assessments made to John and Wm. B. Adams, $3.85; Stephen Brown, $20.79; Jos. O. Clarke and wife 1 cent; Alvah Mowry, 1 cent; R. & Dennis Mowry, $7.70; D. S. Mowry, 1 cent; Daniel Mathewson, $2.12; E. Mathewson, $2.12; W. Mathewson, $2.12; John Mathewson, $5.00; heirs of Syria Steere, $13.86; Elma Steere, $1.62; Alice Steere, $1.62; Nelson Steere, $5.39; Lillis Steere, Taft farm, $6.16—in all $76.35, was collected, and both of the above sums were paid into the hands of the district treasurer, amounting to $306.30.

Owing to alleged illegalities in the assessment of this tax, the collector refused to proceed and collect the balance, and this sum of $306.30 has since remained in the hands of the treasurer of the district.

As the district was owing several sums of money to sundry persons, a meeting was legally called on the 29th day of March, 1856, and was continued by adjournment to April 12th, 1856, for the purpose of paying these debts. At this first meeting it was voted or declared to be the vote of the meeting to pay the debts of the district with the above-named money in the hands of the treasurer. From this vote an appeal is taken, and it is claimed that no persons have the right to vote on questions concerning the disposition or disbursement of this money except such as have paid a portion of it.

The commissioner decides that the school law does imperatively prohibit any person from voting on any question concerning taxation, unless he has paid or shall be liable to pay, a portion of such tax : and on examination of the names of persons who voted for and against said motion to pay the debts of the district with this money, he finds that no person so having paid a portion of said tax, voted in the affirmative, and that five persons so having paid a portion of said tax voted in the negative. He therefore declares that the motion was lost.

At the adjourned meeting held on the 12th of April, it was moved to rescind this vote declared passed at the meeting of the 29th of March. But as that was not carried legally, the rescinding could have no effect.

At a meeting held on the first Monday of May, 1856, it was moved and seconded " that the money that was collected in 1853 and 1854 from the ratable property of a portion of the tax-payers in this district, and paid into the treasury, be paid back to those from whom it was collected." This motion was voted on, and, on an examination of the names of the persons voting, the commissioner finds that nine only had a right, under the school law, to vote ; and that of those voting in the negative, none had a right to vote ; and it is therefore decided that said motion should have been declared to be carried in the affirmative, and it is hereby so decided.

The commissioner therefore decides that said vote to pay the above-named sums of money to the above-named persons who paid them into the treasury of the said District No. 7, was properly and legally carried in the meeting of the voters of the said district, held on the first Monday of May, 1856. And the treasurer of the said district is hereby required and commanded to pay the above-named sums to the persons named in connection therewith.

Give at this office of commissioner of public schools, this 5th day of July, 1856.

ROBERT ALLYN, *Comm'r of Public Schools.*

DECISION No. 27.

In case of the appeal of Philip B. Stiness, Jr., from the act of John H. Willard, clerk of the school committee of North Providence, in ordering sundry bills to be paid to teachers in School District No. 3, of said town, while a protest against the payment of said bills was before the school committee.

This appeal was received June 19, 1856, and sets forth, as a fact, that John H. Willard, as clerk of the school committee of North Providence, made three orders on the town treasury of said town, for certain bills for the wages of the public school teachers in School District No. 3, of said town, while a protest was on record against their payment; that said teachers had not been employed in a legal manner by the trustees of said district, inasmuch as there had been no meeting of the board of trustees for the district, and that at the time of ordering those bills the said J. H. Willard was not legally authorized to order bills for such services, inasmuch as the term of his office had expired.

The appeal was heard on the 21st of June at the office of the commissioner in Providence, Mr. Stiness appearing for his own appeal, and Mr. Willard appearing in opposition to it. The facts were substantially agreed to by the parties, and were as follows, namely:

At the annual district meeting of this School District No. 3, North Providence, in May, 1855, three trustees were elected; one of these resigned sometime in September, 1855. His resignation was accepted by the district in February, 1856, and a new trustee was chosen in his place. The other two trustees refused to recognize the election of this man, and held no meeting of the board of trustees; and it was subsequently decided by the commissioner that said election in February was illegal. The law makes it necessary to have one or three trustees, and as there were but two who were clearly elected legally, the two could not act, especially when they were neglecting to recognize one who had been chosen in a district meeting and held *primâ facie* evidence of being a trustee. The two trustees, therefore, acted in concert, and engaged teachers, though there is no evidence of having called a meeting of their board.

The spring vacation occurred from April 11th to April 28th, or thereabouts, and the summer term commenced on this latter day. The bills paid, or ordered to be paid, were for the wages of the five teachers from this last-named day, up to May 31, 1856, and of course covered more than one month, or one-third of the term. They were presented at the last meeting of the old school committee for the year ending June 2, 1856, and in consequence of the protest above alluded to, the bills were laid over to another meeting. Soon after this last meeting a town meeting was held about June 2d, and a new committee was elected. On the 6th of June the clerk of the old committee, John H. Willard, did give orders for three bills, notwithstanding the protest, the expiration of the year, and the election of a new committee. The amount of these bills is not at all essential to the decision.

Mr. Willard contended that he, as clerk, held office, as did the school committee, till their successors are qualified by taking the engagement, and that school teachers being, as these were said to have been, hired for no definite time, must hold their places till the trustees hire others, or rather till they are dismissed in a legal way.

There are three questions raised for decision in this case:

1. Were these teachers, employed as they must have been on a new term commencing within one of the months fixed for the annual meeting—say April 28th—legally employed, and were they entitled to their wages without some action of the board of trustees or the school committee?

2. Could a clerk of a school committee legally assume the power to order such bills as were under protest, and while thus under protest, having been laid over, either by vote or by consent of the committee, to another meeting, even though he had a general authority to order ordinary bills?

3. And granting that these school teachers were legally employed, and that the clerk would have authority to order bills while under protest and laid over, would he have such authority beyond the year for which he was chosen, and after another committee had been chosen?

The commissioner's opinion upon the first point is, that these teachers were not legally employed. The time of the annual spring vacation in these schools comes within the month of April, a month in which the annual meeting of the district may occur. This must be reckoned the end of their year, unless by special or implied agreement. There was a vacation, and the trustees or the school committee are the only authority to regulate the length of that vacation, and consequently one or the other of these bodies must fix the beginning of the term after that vacation. The trustees could not have done that legally, for they had no legal meeting during the time from March till May 27th, or about that time. And the school committee did not fix the time of commencing these schools. The teachers must therefore be considered as having begun the schools of their own motion, and they were therefore not legally employed in such sense as to be entitled to orders on the town treasury for teachers' money for their wages. It may here be remarked, that as the time from April 28th to May 31st was only a small portion of the summer term, there was ample time for an election of trustees by the district, and the adoption of these schools both by these trustees and the school committee, but at the time of ordering these bills they had not thus been adopted.

As to the second point, whether the clerk could legally order bills of this kind, the commissioner is clearly of opinion, in accordance with a decision of the late commissioner, Hon. E. R. Potter, that the clerk has no power whatever to do any act that is discretionary with the committee to do or not to do. It is a well settled principle that such a body as a school committee cannot delegate to any one of its servants any discretionary power. It may, and indeed will, often find it necessary to delegate ministerial powers, but it cannot go further than this in its acts of delegation. As these bills were under protest, and as it lay wholly in the discretion of the school committee to receive the schools and visit them and allow the teacher their bills for wages, in short, to make them legal, it must be held that any act of the clerk which should attempt to forestall the action of the committee in regard to that protest would be illegal and void.

In regard to the third point, it may be remarked that this need not be decided as material to the case, for the above conclusions arrived at on the first two points will definitely settle the question in all its practical bearings. But inasmuch as it is a point that may be of much practical moment, it is thought best to give an opinion on that also. It seems manifest from the law that it was not intended that a school committee should hold office beyond the time of the appointment of other persons in their place, not the qualification of their successor in office. The 8th section provides for the election of a school committee by the town at its annual meeting, but the town council may appoint the school committee if the town fails to do so, (see Digest, p. 302, section 5 ;) and the filling of vacancies is committed to the board of school committee by section 18. Section 63 declares that all school officers shall hold office till the next annual election or appointment for such office, and until other persons are appointed in their places. And it provides that if any one neglects to take the engagement, he may be fined one dollar ; but all acts of such officers otherwise lawful shall be valid from the time of their election or appointment, notwithstanding such neglect. And this view is still further strengthened by the 18th section, which gives the school committee power to fill vacancies occasioned " by declining to serve." If it requires the engagement of a new officer or school-committee man, in place of the old, to terminate the former's term of office, how can a vacancy occur by declining to serve, as distinct from resignation? A town might decide to remove the old board, but by two members of the new board simply declining to take the oath, the majority of the old board would hold over. It cannot, therefore, be supposed that the law means any thing other than what it plainly says in section 63, that the election or appointment of another person in place of an incumbent in the office of a school committee does necessarily terminate the official term of that incumbent, without waiting for that successor to take his engagement. In a case of so much importance as this, nothing must be presumed that is not specially said in the law ; and as this law does say appointment and not engagement, it must be held that the appointment of a new committee does terminate the term of the old.

A school committee should therefore on no account assume to transact any business after their successors are chosen. An l if they ought not to do this, how much stronger is the reason why the clerk should not attempt an act which lies not at all in his power at any time, but is discretionary with the full board of the committee?

The act of John H. Willard, above recited, is therefore hereby declared to have been wholly illegal, and is therefore declared to be void.

Given at the office of commissioner of public schools, in Providence, this 5th day of July, A. D. 1856.

ROBERT ALLYN, *Comm'r of Public Schools.*

DECISION No. 28.

CASE OF SCHOOL DISTRICT NUMBER SEVEN, TOWN OF WARWICK.

Legality of giving a district tax to a town collector when there is a district collector duly appointed and qualified.

66. " By a vote of School District No. 7, of Warwick, R. I., the undersigned were appointed a committee to submit to the commissioner of public schools the question of the legality of putting the

18

collection of the district tax into the hands of the town collector, together with the records or a copy thereof of the proceedings of the last annual meeting and of all subsequent meetings. They now ask leave to present their case by testimony and argument, and ask that the decision of the commissioner when made, and a statement of the facts as in evidence, shall be laid before the chief justice of the supreme court, for his approval.

To the Commissioner of Public Schools.

HENRY L. GREENE,
WM. B. SPENCER,   } Committee.
JAMES P. GARDNER,

Providence, R. I., October 15, 1856.

Office of Commissioner of Public Schools,
Providence, Oct. 17, 1856.

Upon the question above recited, and upon the evidence produced on the hearing of the same before me, I decide, that, according to the 37th section of the act relating to public schools, "any district may vote to place the collection of any tax or rate bill in the hands of the collector of town taxes," notwithstanding there be a district collector; and I, having been satisfied by evidence that a vote to that effect has been passed at a regular district meeting of School District No. 7, of the town of Warwick, decide that the collection of the tax in question may be legally confided to the collector of town taxes of that town.

Given under my hand the day above named, Oct. 17, 1856.

ROBERT ALLYN, *Comm'r of Public Schools.*

Upon conference with the school commissioner, and a statement of the facts in the above matter by him laid before me, I approve of the above decision.

SAMUEL AMES, *Chief Justice Sup. Court.*

October 17, 1856.

DECISION No. 29.

CASE OF JOSEPH CRANDALL'S APPEAL FROM ACTION OF TRUSTEES OF
SCHOOL DISTRICT NO. 2, EXETER.

Where land lying in two districts is assessed in one parcel by town assessors, trustees of a school district have no right to assess its value, and must call on a town assessor.

Statement and decision of commissioner of public schools in case of the appeal of Joseph Crandall, of Richmond, from the action of the trustees of School District No. 2, of Exeter, in assessing a tax for repairing the school-house in said district. This appeal was made to the commissioner of public schools on the 14th of February, 1857, and was tried at Richmond, on the 10th day of March, 1857. The appellant was heard by counsel George H. Olney, and the trustees by counsel Isaac Greene.

The facts as ascertained by the commissioner, are as follows; and they are reported to Hon. Chief Justice Ames, for his opinion on them, at the joint request of the parties, namely:

On the 30th day of August, 1856, at a legal meeting of the voters of the above-named district, it was voted to assess a tax of $150 on the ratable property of the district. This tax was assessed during the month of November, 1856; and on the 7th of February, 1857, the trustees issued a warrant to collect it.

Among the persons taxed for real estate, was Joseph Crandall, who is owner of two farms in Exeter, one called the "Rathbun farm," lying on the north side of the so-called "Ten-rod road;" the other, called the "Hazard farm," lying adjacent to the Rathbun farm, but on the south side of the said road. This road divides the two districts No. 1 and No. 2,—the latter being on the north, and of course including only the Rathbun farm. It appears that a part of the Hazard farm adjacent to the Rathbun land has for several years been rented with this Rathbun farm; and as the tenant was to pay road taxes, it has been by the town assessors taxed or valued in the same parcel with it.

The tax against which complaint is made was for this parcel of land, which, on the assessors' book for 1855, the book by which the trustees were governed in their assessment, was called the "Rathbun land," and was valued at $900 under their rules. The sum assessed was $12.30.

The appellant claims that this parcel of land, so valued at $900, includes a part of the Hazard farm, lying in another school district, and liable to a tax there ; and that said tax cannot be legal, inasmuch as the trustees did not, in making the assessment, proceed according to the requirements of section 45 of the act relating to public schools, which declares that, in cases of property lying in two districts, and having no separate values on its respective parts, the trustees, if they cannot agree with the owners, shall call on a town assessor, who shall assess the value of the property so situated.

The only question, then, to be decided is a question of fact, as to whether the parcel of land named in the assessors' tax book of 1855, and in the trustees' warrant called the "Rathbun land," is situated wholly within the boundaries of School District No. 2, or partly also in No. 1.

The facts bearing on this question are these : In 1849, the two farms are taxed for the value of $1,800,—Rathbun farm, $600 ; Hazard farm, $1,200 ; and this valuation has not materially changed since, though diminished a trifle.   In 1853, there is a different division of values,—the Rathbun farm being set at $900, and the Hazard farm at $850.   This division of values continued to 1856, when it stands,—Rathbun, $667 ; Hazard, in two parcels $1,002.   So much for the testimony obtained from the town assessors' tax books.

Mr. Edward Barber of S., assessor of taxes for the town of Exeter, testified as to the respective values, and as to the situation of the two farms, and as to the assessment on the Rathbun land, stating that the value on the tax-book of 1855, was understood by him to be for the whole of the Rathbun land, and also for all that part of the Hazard farm east of Parish Brook, so called ; and that the value of the Rathbun farm, according to their mode of computing, was about $600.

The commissioner, therefore, cannot doubt that the aforenamed sum of $900, taxed as the value of the "Rathbun land," does include the value of a part of the "Hazard farm," which lies without the bounds of this District No. 2, and which, in his opinion, ought not to have been taxed.

As this is one of the cases specially provided for in section 45, above referred to, in which a town assessor ought to have been called in to apportion the value of the land thus situated in two adjoining districts, and as the tax was assessed by the trustees instead of the assessor, contrary to the requirements of the statute, the commissioner is of opinion that the tax appealed from was illegally assessed ; and the assessment is therefore hereby declared void.

Give at the office of commissioner of public schools, in Providence, this 31st day of March, 1857.

ROBERT ALLYN, *Comm'r of Public Schools.*

Upon the statement of facts above named, I approve of the decision of the commissioner.

SAMUEL AMES, *Chief Justice Supreme Court.*

Providence, April 21, 1857.

DECISION No. 30.

CASE OF APPEAL OF JOHN H. WILLARD.

School committee cannot vacate the office of clerk but by hearing and for cause.

Statement and decision of commissioner of public schools in case of appeal of John H. Willard, from a vote of the school committee of North Providence, declaring the office of the clerk of their board vacant, passed December 13, 1856.

The facts in this case are as follows, namely:

On the 13th of December, 1856, at the regular monthly meeting of the school committee of North Providence, a resolution was offered, and passed in these words: " Whereas, the clerk refuses to complete the record of July 19, 1856, as voted at this meeting of the school committee, December 13, 1856, therefore, *Resolved,* That the office of the clerk be declared vacant." P. B. Stiness, Jr., was then elected clerk to fill the vacancy thus created; and John H. Willard, the appellant, who had been elected clerk of the committee at their first special meeting, held June 14, 1856, gave notice of his intention to appeal to the commissioner of public schools from the vote declaring his office vacant.

The appeal was accordingly made December 15, 1856, and received by the commissioner on the 17th; and by notice given to the parties on the 17th, the time of hearing was fixed on December 20th, at two o'clock, P. M., at the commissioner's office in Providence.

On the trial the parties appeared, and were heard by testimony and argument before the commissioner.

The points raised for consideration are two. 1. Has the school committee a right, after having made an election of a clerk,—an officer created by the school law and necessary to the organization and legal action of the committee,—to remove that clerk, unless by charges and trial, after notice, for misdemeanor before the expiration of the term of their office ?

2. If they have such right or power, were the reasons alleged sufficient to justify them in the summary exercise of that right ?

If the first question be decided in the negative, there is no occasion to examine the testimony upon the second.

I am of opinion that the school law, (see sections 9 and 10,) makes the election of a chairman and clerk necessary to a legal organization of the committee, and the law nowhere gives to the committee any power whatever to remove its officers. This removal can therefore only be made for cause, and in the same manner as any other officer elected for a specified time could be removed. This must be by trial, and after notice.

With this view, a decision of the late commissioner, Hon. E. R. Potter, accords. That was in regard to a district trustee, an officer of no more responsibility than a clerk of the school committee, and was to the effect that " an election once made could not be rescinded, and that he, the trustee, could only be removed after notice and a hearing."

My decision, therefore, is, that said vote, passed as it was without previous notice and opportunity given for hearing and trial, is void.

By request of Mr. Willard, made on the hearing before me, this decision is now submitted to his honor, Chief Justice Ames, of the supreme court, for his opinion thereon.

Given under my hand, at the office of commissioner of public schools in Providence, this 31st of January, A. D. 1857.

ROBERT ALLYN, *Comm'r of Public Schools.*

OPINION OF THE SUPREME COURT.

Upon the annexed statement of facts, understanding as I do from it that the school committee of North Providence declared the office of clerk of their board vacant without notice to the clerk of the charges against him, and without affording him an opportunity by proof and agreement to defend himself,

I am of opinion, and decide, that said vote was void, and that John H. Willard is therefore legally clerk of said board.

If Mr. Willard being present asked no delay, but proceeded to defend himself, he would be deemed to have waived formal notice, and the vote would be valid.

As nothing of this kind is stated in the annexed statement of facts, I presume the contrary to be true, and this renders it unnecessary for me to examine into the second question stated by the commissioner.

SAMUEL AMES, *C. J. Supreme Court.*

Providence, January 31, 1857.

DECISION No. 31.

CASE OF J. H. WILLARD, CLERK, REMOVED.

A clerk of a school committee may be removed from office for cause, after notice and hearing.

Statement and decision in case of the appeal of John H. Willard from a vote of the school committee of North Providence; by which they declared his office, as clerk of said committee, vacant.

This appeal was received at the office of the commissioner of public schools on the 27th of March, 1857. It is directed to the commissioner, and sets forth the fact, that, on the 21st day of March, 1857, the school committee of North Providence did, by resolution, declare vacant the office of clerk of their board, at that time held by the appellant, John H. Willard, for the reasons set forth in the said resolution; that said Willard had refused to present a certain paper to the board when demanded by vote of the committee; that he refused or failed to make certain corrections or additions to the records of said committee, when ordered by their vote; that he had used improper language to the members of said committee at their meetings, and for other matters alleged. The appeal alleges that these charges are false and malicious, and also claims that the committee have no legal authority to remove a clerk.

The hearing was appointed for April 13th, at which time the parties appeared at the office of the commissioner of public schools, and a full hearing of the case was had.

Mr. Willard appeared in behalf of his appeal, and Mr. Stiness for the school committee. Much testimony was introduced, and much of it was conflicting. These are the facts, as they appear to the commissioner to have been proved in the case.

Sometime in July, 1856, a paper was sent from the commissioner of public schools to the school committee of North Providence, through their clerk, Mr. Willard, with a request that he would communicate it to the board. When the board met this paper was called for, and Mr. Willard did not produce it. A vote was passed demanding it; still it was not produced, and the committee adjourned without it. At a subsequent meeting it was given to the committee. Mr. Willard attempted on the trial to show that he might choose his own time to produce it, and that his refusal was only a qualified one. On this point the commissioner is clearly of opinion that the clerk of a board like a school committee, has no discretion whatever in such cases. The records and papers are not his private property, but belong to the committee, and he only has charge of them, and holds them entirely subject to their order. It was said that the paper in question was one that would prevent some action of the committee, and would in some respects damage the reputation of the commissioner. But the clerk of a school committee is not the judge of the duties and business of the committee, nor the custodian of the commissioner's reputation. If the committee demanded a paper belonging to them, and insisted on that demand, it was the clerk's duty to present it, no matter what business might be prevented or cut off by it, and no matter whose reputation might be hurt.

The next matter in the resolution from which the appeal was taken, related to the refusal of the clerk to amend the records of the meeting at which the above-named paper was demanded. It appears by the clerk's records, that at the next meeting the record of the meeting above-named was not approved, on account of its imperfection. A motion to amend, by inserting the words " which was refused," and which would have made the records accord with the truth, was laid on the table, in the hope that after consideration the clerk would make the proper amendment. In December, however, the amendment not having been made, a vote was passed to amend as above stated, and the clerk refused to amend. He contends that his refusal was only conditional, — he being willing to add after the words " that the clerk be directed to produce the decision of the commissioner," these other words, " which was refused," provided he could spread his reasons for refusing on the records of the committee. No vote was taken by the committee to prevent this putting his reasons on record ; and the clerk appears never to have made any such proposal to the committee, except in the intervals of a very angry and excited personal controversy with the chairman and others Neither did he ask the privilege of writing out his reasons, and placing them on file with the decision of the commissioner, which had never been recorded. The books of the committee show that the required correction has never been made; and as the committee, and not the clerk, are responsible for the accuracy of these records after their approval by themselves, and especially after they by vote direct them to be amended, the commissioner must consider it a fact proved, that the clerk did refuse to amend the records, according to the facts, as he was required to do by vote of the school committee.

As to the matter of improper language used by the clerk to the committee, the commissioner will dismiss it entirely, simply remarking, that the testimony goes to show that Mr. Willard is only one of those who may have used words unbecoming the dignity of those who have the guardianship of our public schools. Undoubtedly, in the angry controversies of the year, all were provoked; and the one who best governed his temper and controlled his tongue, certainly has more to feel proud of, than he who excelled in the harshness and coarseness of the epithets applied to his fellows.

The resolution appealed from contained other allegations, which it is not necessary to consider, since the first two above recited are sufficient, and are in fact all that is really essential to the case.

Mr. Willard contended that the charges above were malicious. But as the facts do clearly show that he did fail to produce the decision, and did also fail to amend the records as directed, it would seem that there could be no malice on the part of the committee. Indeed, it was clearly established that the resolutions making the vacancy were passed by a vote of six to two,— Mr. Willard himself voting with the minority. The only indication of ill-will is found in the fact, that the committee allowed so much time to elapse,—from July to March—before taking energetic measures to maintain their own rights in the matter. But this is accounted for by the fact, that they were hoping for a peaceable arrangement until December, when they passed a vote similar to the resolution under consideration, from which an appeal was taken, and Mr. Willard was reïnstated because of a deficiency in proving the notice of the intention of the committee to pass the vote of removal from office. The commissioner could discover no evidence whatever of malice on the part of the committee as a body.

Mr. Willard also claimed that the resolutions were false, since he had only, as his argument stated, refused with a qualification to perform what was required. But, whatever qualifications might have been made, or whatever favors were or were not asked by the clerk, they were not allowed by the committee; and as the records are still imperfect, it must be held that there was a refusal, in act at least, to perform a duty specially prescribed by vote of the committee, and that the committee have the right to seek other instruments to carry out their wishes.

Mr. Willard further in his argument contends that no power is given in the school laws to the committee to remove a clerk, and that such an officer can be removed only by impeachment; but section sixty-five of the law, to which reference is made, speaks of penalties for the non-performance or mal-performance of duties by school officers, and does not mention removal from office. There is a wide difference between removal from office, and punishment inflicted for wilful crime in office. As removal is not mentioned in the law, this must, when deemed necessary, be done in accordance with common law. A decision was made by the late commissioner, Hon. E. R. Potter, in relation to the removal of trustees, in which he says, " they can only be removed after notice and trial for cause ;" and this implies that these and other school officers can be removed, by the bodies appointing them, after such notice and trial, for cause. An opinion given by Chief Justice Ames on January 31, 1857, is to the purport that a clerk of a school committee can be lawfully removed for good cause, after notice and trial. Another opinion, given by the same judge in case of Smith, asking a rehearing before the commissioner, implies that the evident design of the school law was to relieve the courts from litigation in the small matters that may concern the public schools, and to provide tribunals, cheap, accessible, and speedy, for the redress of wrong or injury in such cases. But if a school committee must be compelled to go before a court of law for redress, in cases of every refractory clerk or other officer elected by them, for the sole purpose of giving expression to, or of recording their doings, this very laudable object of the law will be entirely defeated. This seems entirely contrary to the whole spirit of the law, and is believed to be contrary to usage also.

It is therefore held, that the committee have power to remove their clerk, after sufficient notice of their intention, and opportunity for trial and defence. That the appellant had such notice and made defence was fully proved. The appellant asks that the facts may be laid before Hon. Chief Justice Ames for his opinion thereon.

It then only remains to consider whether the causes alleged for removal, as above recited, were true, and sufficient to warrant the action of the committee. And the commissioner decides that in his opinion they were fully proved to be true, as above stated, and that they were also sufficient to warrant the removal.

The vote or resolution is therefore hereby affirmed, and it is declared, that the office of clerk of the school committee of North Providence, lately held by John H. Willard, is vacant.

Given at the office of commissioner of public schools, in Providence, April 18, 1857.

ROBERT ALLYN, *Comm'r of Public Schools.*

Upon appeal of John H. Willard from vote of school committee of North Providence, removing him from the office of clerk of said committee.

I fully concur in the above opinion of the commissioner as to the power of the school committee of a town to remove their clerk for just cause after hearing, full opportunity having been given to him upon charges presented to defend himself against them. Such a power, with regard to such an officer, unless expressly forbidden by law, is incidental to the committee as necessary to enable it duly to perform its functions.

Upon the statement of facts above made, from the testimony by the commissioner, I fully concur with him that a just and legal cause for the removal of John H. Willard, as clerk of the school committee of North Providence, was shown by the committee for their action in the case of the appellant, and do therefore approve his decision on this appeal.

SAMUEL AMES, *Chief Justice Supreme Court of R. I., &c.*

Providence, April 18, 1857.

DECISION No. 32.

GENERAL INSTRUCTIONS.

To School Committees and Superintendents of Towns, Trustees of Districts, and Teachers and Candidates for the office of Teacher.

Representations have often been made to the commissioner of public schools, by many friends of public education and common schools in various parts of the state, that it is not uncommon for teachers to be employed by trustees to keep a school in the district of which they are officers, and to commence schools in such districts without certificates of qualifications from the examiners of the town. It has further been represented that the trustee of a district sometimes employs a teacher having a certificate from the school committee, the year of which has not expired, or one who has a county or state certificate, and having employed such an one, authorizes him to begin school, and neglects to notify the visiting committee or superintendent of the town when the school is to begin ; thereby depriving them (unless accident gives such information) of the power to visit the school within two weeks of its beginning, as the law imperatively requires.

Under this representation of facts which are believed to be undisputed and altogether too common, and which are understood to be too easily excused and overlooked by the proper authorities, it becomes the duty of the commissioner of public schools to call attention to the plain and positive requirements of the law in such cases.

1st. A teacher without a certificate can in no case be legally paid for his services out of the public money, no matter how well qualified he may be, nor how well he may have taught and governed his school ;—and every officer who draws an order, or uses the public money to pay him, is liable to indictment and fine.

2d. No school is legally kept, unless it be visited TWICE, at least, by the school committee, or by some person by them appointed, or by the superintendent of the town,—once within two weeks of its commencement, and once within two weeks of its close. And if the officer whose duty it is to visit fail of discharging that duty, he is liable to suit at law ; and if the trustee neglect his duty in the matter of giving information as to the time of commencing or closing the school, he is also liable at law.

These things ought to engage the attention of all friends of public schools. They are more than mere forms. They involve the whole system of supervising our schools, and of course connect themselves with all the details and practical operations of public education. And the law, in these essentially vital points, should be scrupulously complied with.

Teachers, therefore, should refuse to begin a school until they have a certificate of qualifications, and the town committee or superintendent has been notified of the time of commencing.

Trustees, also, should insist that the teacher shall be examined immediately after his employment, and always before he enters the school-room for the purpose of teaching; and they should be very punctilious about giving notice to the committee or superintendent, of the time of beginning and closing the schools.

And school committees, examiners, visitors, and superintendents should stand on the extreme limit of the law, insisting that they will give no orders in favor of a teacher, trustee, or district, where there has been a neglect, in any way, or on any account, to comply with these simple and just, as well as prudent and wholesome, requirements of the law.

ROBERT ALLYN, *Comm'r of Pub. Schools.*

DECISION No. 33.

CASE OF W. S. HOLT, SCHOOL DISTRICT, NUMBER ELEVEN, EXETER.

A tax approved by the School Committee if subsequently increased, must be again approved. A trustee not authorized to insure a School-House, without authority from the District.

The facts appear to be the following: District No. 11 in the town of Exeter, voted to raise a tax of one hundred and fifty dollars for the purpose of repairing their school-house. This meeting was held Oct. 9, 1858. The trustee and clerk were appointed to make the repairs. These repairs were accordingly made, and the house insured, without any vote of the district authorizing it.

At a meeting of the district held Nov. 6, 1858, it was voted to receive the house and assess a tax of one hundred and eighty-six dollars, and some cents. From this vote, Mr. Holt appealed to the commissioner. Having appointed a hearing at the school-house of said district, Dec. 22, 1858, Mr. Holt made the following points of objection. That the original vote limited the tax to *one hundred and fifty dollars;* that the notice of the second meeting was illegal, inasmuch as it did not state that a sum greater than one hundred and fifty dollars was to be raised ; that only the sum of one hundred and fifty dollars had been approved by the school committee; that the expenses had been increased by ceiling the walls of the school-house below the windows, when the district had voted not to ceil them ; that the expenses had been increased by the amount paid for the insurance ; that all the bills were not presented when the vote to assess a tax was passed ; and that the repairs had cost too much.

Only three of these points of objection can be sustained. The " notice " of the second meeting, the approval of the school committee, and the insurance. The " notice " and " insurance " may be reduced to one. The power to insure a school-house is by Sec. 3, Chap. 61, School Law, vested in the district and not in the trustee. Yet, if the " notice " had specified insurance as one of the objects of the meeting, a vote of the district, sanctioning the trustee, would have been legal.

It is my opinion and decision that this tax is not legal,—because the whole tax has not been approved by the school-committee, and the notice not sufficient to authorize the district to sanction the act of the trustee in procuring insurance on the house.

JOHN KINGSBURY, *Comm'r of Public Schools.*

DECISION No. 34.

CASE OF SCHOOL DISTRICT NUMBER ONE, BARRINGTON.

A School-House may be occupied for a Signing School, when such occupation does not interfere with the ordinary school.

The following appear to be the facts in the case. Mr. Christopher Roffee is occupying the school-house of district No. 1, in the town of Barrington, by permission of the trustees of said district, as appears by the accompanying certificate of one of the trustees for the purpose of giving instruction in vocal music.

At a legally notified meeting of the tax paying voters of said district, held Feb. 3d, 1860, the following vote, as certified to by the clerk of said district, was negatived "that the district school-house shall be used for no other purpose than public school and district purpose."

From what purports to be said vote, John W. Barnes appealed, with a request that a statement of the facts in the case might be laid before one of the Justices of the Supreme Court for decision.

After due consideration, I am compelled to dismiss the appeal of said Barnes, without further hearing, and for the following reasons:

Because, the vote as quoted in your appeal is not the vote negatived at said meeting, as certified to by the district clerk. *Because,* the vote, certified to as negatived at said meeting is inoperative ; inasmuch as the school law has already been interpreted to allow a district school-house to be used for purposes not necessarily " district," viz. : for lyceums, debating societies, lectures and other matters connected with education. (See Decision No. 10, under School Laws.)

The question at issue is manifestly without the jurisdiction of the district, and has already been decided upon by the proper tribunal, viz. : by the commissioner of public schools, approved by the Chief Justice of the Supreme Court.

With regard to the instance cited in said appeal, as a violation of such decision, I am of opinion that the use of said house for such instruction is perfectly legitimate " to purposes connected with public instruction."

Instruction in vocal music, is a part of our system of public education, and is so recognized and paid for by the city of Providence, out of the "teachers' money," and is recognized and employed as an important element of education in nearly all the rural districts of our commonwealth. Many of our school committees insist upon its introduction into the public schools, and nearly all the school reports which reach the office, are emphatic in its recommendation. And certainly if the younger children may be instructed in vocal music in the public school-house, and this too during school hours, there can be no legal objection why their older brothers and sisters and friends may not receive such instruction at the same place, out of school hours.

Nor is the fact that the teacher receives pecuniary compensation from his pupils, pertinent to the question ; for to allow it to be so, would be to question the legal use of school-houses for public schools, many of the sessions of which are prolonged by *private* subscriptions, and are of course kept in the same sense in which the one is kept to which reference is made, by " private " individuals.

The manner in which any teacher is paid, or whether his services are gratuitous, does not affect the question in point. Moreover, such a legitimate use of the school-house would not require " the general consent of the tax-paying voters," said " private individual " having permission for occupancy from the trustees of said district, in whom the law places the custody of the school-house. (See chapter 65, section 1, revised statutes.)

J. B. CHAPIN, *Comm'r of Public Schools.*

Providence, Feb. 14, 1860.

INDEX.

c. stands for chapter. s. for section of the school law, and p. for page.

20

www.ingramcontent.com/pod-product-compliance
Lightning Source LLC
Chambersburg PA
CBHW030551040726
47497CB00008B/2677